HOW TO BE A
REVOLUTIONARY

HOW TO BE A
REVOLUTIONARY

A Novel

by C. A. Davids

VERSO
London • New York

First published by Verso 2021
© C. A. Davids 2021

1 3 5 7 9 10 8 6 4 2

Verso
UK: 6 Meard Street, London W1F 0EG
US: 20 Jay Street, Suite 1010, Brooklyn, NY 11201
versobooks.com

Verso is the imprint of New Left Books

ISBN-13: 978-1-83976-087-7
ISBN-13: 978-1-83976-088-4 (UK EBK)
ISBN-13: 978-1-83976-089-1 (US EBK)

British Library Cataloguing in Publication Data
A catalogue record for this book is available from the British Library

Library of Congress Cataloging-in-Publication Data
Library of Congress Control Number: 2021940994

Typeset in Electra by Biblichor Ltd, Edinburgh
Printed and bound by CPI Group (UK) Ltd, Croydon CR0 4YY

To those who walked beside me:
My grandmother, Florence
My uncle, Gerald

My husband, Micah

And to Zenda, Rejane and Crystal

"I'll love you, dear, I'll love you
 Till China and Africa meet
And the river jumps over the mountain
 And the salmon sing in the street."

"As I walked out one evening," W. H. Auden

1

SHANGHAI

The repetitive beat of typewriter keys always amplified at around one a.m., because this was the time when life on the street below stilled. Shanghai never became truly quiet. Only in the slip of time between midnight and four a.m. did the traffic recede and the noise temporarily wane. All day long the din of construction filled the air as cranes and gantries, as common to the sky as birds and planes to other cities, crisscrossed the grey. Bamboo scaffolding woven intricately as fine cotton gave shape to the vertical city, while beneath, shift workers arrived all day long, the hum and thrust of metal always in the distance.

In those months when I was new to the city and its unfathomable sounds, I knew this was the time, if any, that I would hear him typing.

The procession of taps and clicks was followed by a quick ring, a slow zip; familiar sounds that had echoed throughout my childhood when my mother brought home extra work. It kept time to my weakening eyelids until, as always, I lost the battle. There was no music now in the beat that seeped through the skin of cement, and I knew my neighbour from above used only one finger. Ayi said he was a man; she'd seen him smoking on the balcony one morning. At least I think she said this. She didn't speak a word of English and I'd learned only the most perfunctory Mandarin: hello, goodbye, thank you, excuse me, how much for that . . . no, that, and so on. A combination of signs, gestures, and incomprehensible words stitched together my and Ayi's communication about the work she had to do when she came to clean. We never said much more, and I only gleaned the bit of information about my neighbour when something crashed one morning in the apartment above, surprising us both. Ayi responded in a stream of furious indignation, gesturing my neighbour's chain smoking and, I guessed, his goatee.

Anyway, I was certain he was a man from the way his pee hit the bowl in a steady hard stream at four a.m.

The typing kept me awake but also strangely comforted. It made up in some small way for the empty space beside me.

~

I had just unpacked the few groceries that I'd bought at the international store: bread, coffee, a bottle of South African wine that I'd already opened, and imported milk (the scandal where melamine had been added to dairy products to increase their weight had only just passed, people had died and everyone was still on edge).

The knocking startled me. No one besides Ayi came to my door, and the roaring bronze lion head above the polished knocker was unused.

"Good evening."

2

Words emerged from the draughty passageway that sounded studied, wooden: ". . . I would appreciate your assistance."

I didn't open the door fully, even though I felt safe in the apartment, in the city.

"You speak English? I am looking for a word please." I opened the door a fraction more so I could see him properly. He must have been in his early sixties I decided from the skein of silver hair that hung around his ears, while his hands, delicate and careful, were cupped before him in a question.

"I'm not sure I understand."

"I am looking for a word . . . something like 'sad,' but not 'sad,'" he said, shaking this idea from his head. "Something more rich."

"You are writing something in English?" I asked. He nodded. ". . . Then it depends how you will use the word. What's the context?" I said, smiling now but maintaining the door at 45 degrees. I was equally perplexed and intrigued by the stranger and wondered why, of all the doors he might have approached, he'd come to mine.

"No . . ." his face broke into a bemused smile, "I am sorry cannot give."

Sometimes it felt as if I were speaking into a body of water here: words spoken but the meaning distorted, warped in translation, even with people who had a strong command of English, so I was learning to adapt.

"I mean to say I need to understand how you will use the word, so I can give you the best one." I tilted my head. He followed suit.

"I understand," he said, "but cannot give."

3

"Well . . . maybe you should come inside," I swung the door fully open, and for months after couldn't say why I'd invited the stranger into my home. I'd made no friends in the city; hadn't even gone to the welcome for new consular staff a few weeks earlier, and I was coming to think of my solitariness as a choice, as a decision.

He made his way into the living room and towards the windows that held the Huangpu River and its smoky vista, a filament of pink dragged right across the sky.

"It's a good view," I said.

"Mine the same," he replied.

"Oh, really, you're in the same block?" I asked, at which he pointed up. "On a higher floor?"

"One up. My view same, but better," he smiled again.

Maybe I'd misunderstood.

"You live above me?"

"Yes, right above. One up," he said, his pointer nudging the air.

My grasp about the man began to solidify: It was him—my inconsiderate neighbour, my pertinacious typist—coming over to ask for a word? I wasn't angry . . . perhaps mildly annoyed but curious; after all, hadn't his life become part of mine, leaking into my sleep, establishing some sense of routine?

I said, "I hear you sometimes."

"What?"

"Typing . . . the typing in the middle of the night." He watched my fingers pounding invisible letters and hitting a nonexistent type bar.

4

"You can hear . . . no, you are mistaken . . ." he stammered. "This is not me. I do not possess."

"Really? But I was certain the sounds were coming from above," I said, bewilderment and, I suppose, an involuntary challenge rising in my voice.

We stared at each other.

Of course I had already been schooled, warned even, about the intricate set of formalities and courtesies that presided over social interactions in China. The city's non-Chinese spoke about face-saving in wary tones; a tower of books had been written about it and the dreadful perils that awaited those who didn't pretend an error or fib or omission or far worse hadn't been seen, though it clearly had been. I'd thought the matter of face-saving exaggerated, dramatized to keep foreigners on their toes. Yet now, confronted with the understanding that offence was about to be caused, or already had been, I felt my face heating, and backtracking, I said in mitigation,

"Erm, you know . . . I'd just opened a bottle of wine when you knocked at the door. Could I offer you a glass . . . we should sit down . . . I can't finish a bottle all by myself." I walked to the kitchen without waiting for his answer.

When I returned to the living room, he was holding a book in his hand. One eye was screwed tight, the other scanning its back as his fingers tiptoed up the spine.

"Oh, that's a book of letters that Langston Hughes wrote . . . actually, to someone from my country," I said, checking the cover. "You know Langston Hughes?"

"Of course, have read."

5

"Oh." I tried not to show how pleased I was; almost irrationally so.

"You from . . . where?"

"South Africa," I said.

He drank the wine quickly, without stopping, and when he was done, said in the practiced tone that I'd first heard at the door, "Thank you for your kindness." He gave a deep nod, almost a bow, and left without waiting for my reply or the word for which he had first come.

~

Do I believe in serendipity? Of course not, and yet I picked *him* out days later. Not in a likely place like the garden or the stairwell, but out there in a city crammed with 22 million human souls. Even in Johannesburg, with a quarter of those numbers, I knew I could go years without bumping into anyone familiar, even a careless husband.

How utterly unprepared I'd been for weekends when infinitely tall, boundless apartment blocks burst, dumping industrious people—contained for the whole week—into the streets, parks and shopping centres with a clamorous joy. That Saturday I couldn't navigate the long avenue to Super Brand Mall, where I'd started going regularly for a meal or to do the weekly shop. In our multitudes, like caravans of shrews, we attached ourselves to someone before or behind us and, in this way, foraged for food and bargains.

The mall was no less jammed, and slowly I felt myself going under, drowning in a tightly packed phalanx of human bodies, more than I had ever seen. I elbowed my way across the mall, peeking into windows as I competed for space and the few breaths of air, until, giving up, I walked out into the hot damp afternoon. I must have walked for five minutes or more, uncertain where I was going but trying only to get ahead of the throngs that knotted everywhere, even at intersections.

I saw him then, standing on the pavement and speaking loudly on an old mobile phone that dwarfed his hand. He was about to enter the city's tallest building. Did I follow him in because I was so sick of my own company already? I let the escalator fill between us, but like everywhere else it was almost impossible to move, and by the time I alighted on the second floor, he was gone.

The building I'd just entered housed one of the priciest hotels in Shanghai. By then I'd already developed a penchant for the mostly grand buildings, discovered on solitary walks. My aimless wanderings allowed me to fit the city together, piecing street to suburb, and to explore the expensive caverns which gave me uninterrupted time to ruminate about my semi-dissolved marriage. I'd only told Andrew about the job one month before moving.

What? Shanghai? But what about my work here?

I didn't think you would want to go with, Andrew, I'd said.

What?

You could stay.

So, what then, we have a long-distance marriage?

I'm not sure that would work.

I'm confused.

I leave next month. We'll sort it out, I said, turning to finish the email I'd started writing.

In the weeks that followed, between his work trips and my preparations, I'd found it easier than I'd imagined—maybe than I'd hoped—to avoid him.

I took an elevator to the 24th floor and sat at the window in the wood-panelled coffee shop of the City International. The only other people were a man and woman, dressed immaculately in designer wear. She: seated beside an angle-poised lamp, diamond clusters on her fingers and ears that hooked stray strands of light, refracted and wrapped the pair in their own glamour. Her face, though, was a mask of modern dermatology and a lifetime of avoiding the sun: creaseless and characterless too. I guessed she was around my age, late thirties or older, from the way her movements were measured, deliberate. He was dressed like an American rapper minus the effortlessness, the street cred: head-to-toe gold and cream logos, the peak of his cap tipped to ten o'clock.

This was the way I occupied my first months in the city. Watching. Waiting, too. What for? I had no idea. Any case, there was nothing to see from the windows but the wide stretch of smog anaesthetizing everything so it was as pallid twenty-odd floors above the world as it was down below. I'd brought my book with me and picked up from where I'd left off.

~

Maybe thirty minutes had passed by the time they walked in: the typist with a younger man. Thunder was stripping the afternoon of its peace and the room had gone a docile sepia; stray arcs of light drifted across the wallpaper. The coffee shop was empty and staff hovered about cleaning up spills, straightening tablecloths and preparing the place for an influx of patrons that I knew, as did they, would not arrive anytime soon.

The men took a table at the other end of the room and ordered tea. Their conversation or rather their argument was so intense, so animated that I could barely look away, for fear that I'd miss some detail that might decode what was happening before me. All the while their bodies jutted and shifted at irregular angles, miming their disagreement. They rose after about ten minutes, tea still unpoured, scraped their chairs (gratuitously?) along the cool marble floors, then turned and without saying another word went their separate ways.

As he passed by our eyes met. My neighbour paused, but he didn't recognize me, or so he pretended.

2

CAPE TOWN

1989

From above the city was a watercolour painted in azure oceans, golden sands, dark emerald forests.

Tourists were resolute in telling Beth that Cape Town was the most beautiful city in all the world, with its curious arrangement of Fynbos flora, its scraggy strange beauty over peaks and plains, the flat mountain, two oceans, its forests, wine farms, charming Victorian buildings. So, so pretty.

What no one said was that over there . . . no, over there, where the eye never falls naturally . . . further still . . . it was nothing but a charcoal sketch. A smudge of humanity.

The dick-shaped map of the Peninsula was indecent, but no local needed a map; it was the city that had shaped their bones, its seawater that ran in their miscegenated veins.

The same tourists—aunties and uncles actually—had long ago joined the run to Melbourne or London or Toronto, leaving apartheid and its low-level war behind them. They only ever returned with new accents for biannual pilgrimages, to remind themselves why they'd left and to gorge on samoosas (no one makes them like this . . . all we see are mince-less pastry hats), bags of chips (we miss it even more than family), biscuits (just not the same back there). The tourists would rearrange your living space while subtly demanding outings to all the beauteous far-flung spots; only remembering when they reached the destination that they still weren't welcome, still weren't allowed because they, like you, were still the same shade of inferior. And when they returned to your unspeakable neighbourhood, hidden like an arsehole, they'd shield their eyes in renewed shame.

So no, no one could tell Beth. She knew everything there was to know about the place. Recreation in the suburb of Water Falls consisted of an embankment beside a lake that washed up dead bodies every month and a post-apocalyptic park with swings that shifted eerily in the breeze, merry-go-rounds that turned with not a person in sight; at least not until sunset, when the zombies, reel-ing on a cocktail of chemicals, emerged to sit in wait for the decent, and certainly, the indecent.

Beth wasn't stupid, not even close. How could anything be yours—say like a city into which you'd been fool enough to be born—intimately yours, and not belong to you at all? The wrongness of it burned.

~

She ran the toe of a dog-chewed takkie along the perimeter of the loose cement block. Beth weighed up whether she should turn back or not. If she went home, she'd have to accept that this had been a failed mission. Shit, who was she to think she could ever be a revolutionary? She'd probably worn the wrong clothes, too: the oldest jeans she had, a red T-shirt she'd found at the back of her cupboard, and the filthiest takkies she owned. Beth worked her foot beneath the loose cement tile and started fiddling, balancing it on her toe before dropping it back down. If she turned her head thirty degrees, she didn't need to look directly at the group to study them at the entrance to the hall. They were the real thing. From a township school, with authentic T-shirts with slogans and everything: *A injury to one is a injury to all*; *Phantsi Bantu Education Phantsi*, above a fisted salute.

Beth was about to walk back to the bus stop, kicking the dirt-brown sand as she'd done all the way there, when she saw a girl she recognized from school seated at the top of a flight of stairs, framed by the wooden doors of the community hall and a dusting of late afternoon light. It took some kind of courage for Beth to walk up to her.

"You going to the meeting?" Beth asked, laid-back as she could.

"Yip. You?" The girl evaluated Beth carefully as she shielded her eyes, a row of black rubber bangles swinging from her wrist to her elbow.

"Same."

"What's your name?"

"Beth."

"You have a entjie, Beth?" she said, beneath steady, charcoal-laden eyes.

"Me? No, I don't smoke," Beth said. "I mean, I smoke sometimes, but I don't carry with me," she added, frisking her pockets as proof, wishing she'd just stopped at no.

The girl was dressed in multicoloured pants that flapped languidly in the midsummer breeze; harem pants, Beth thought, matched with a bright orange vest. Her hair was cut as short as a boy's and her arm rested on a pile of books beside her.

"What you reading?" said Beth, who might have walked away, had she not found herself incomprehensibly rooted to the spot.

"Things I found at the school library. Mrs. Adams is oulams, she won't let us take more than three books," the girl said, and showed Beth the covers. Oswald Mtshali's poetry, some sort of a pamphlet, and *Buckingham Palace, District Six* by Richard Rive.

"Isn't that book by Rive banned?" Beth said, swallowing a gasp.

"Dunno . . . maybe," the girl said, "Anyway, what you doing here? I never imagined I'd see anyone else from school."

Beth straightened her back against the girl's gaze. Didn't she know she was wearing the wrong outfit entirely to be a revolutionary?

"Saw a poster at school. Took some doing to get where it'd be held from the comrades smoking at the back of the school," Beth said.

"What, people actually read the posters?"

"Wait . . . you're the one that pastes them everywhere . . ." Beth said, forgetting to disguise a tone of awe. The posters had become a site of conflict at Water Falls High. Despite Principal Salie's decree that nothing was to be stuck onto the school walls that ruined the façade, the notices reappeared regularly, stealthily.

"Ja, but you gotta keep it a secret between us. This shit can get a girl killed. I'm kak scared of the boere . . . and also Salie," she added, laughing, so Beth noticed her uneven smile that stretched

14

to below her cheekbone on one side, stopping far short on the other.

"I'm kak impressed," Beth said, loosening her tongue, catching on fast.

"Toss for secret." She offered her small finger.

"Toss. Are you going in?" asked Beth, who was sure she'd felt a quiver run through her pinkie as the girls locked.

"Ja, but they always late. The township comrades have to travel far when the meetings are held this side."

"Sure," Beth said, nodding so hard her neck started to ache.

"And sometimes they have to walk deurmekaar to get to a meeting. Throw the cops off their scent. Walk one by one from the station, take different routes."

"Obviously."

A rowdy group came around the corner just then in complete defiance of what the girl had said, filtering in through the door as many as would fit at the same time.

"Comrades . . . discipline!" She shouted after them.

"You know them?" Beth asked.

"Come," she said, rising and following the group into a small room at the side of the community hall.

"Check you later." She directed Beth to a chair beside a boy wearing an oversized green jersey in the process of unknitting itself at the cuffs and collar. "We can take the bus back to Water Falls together." Beth nodded dutifully, not even bothering to fight the sense of wonder that was now creeping up her back.

The girl did a rough count of everyone, jotted it into a black hardcover book, and when she had finished raised her fist high into the air: "Amaaaandla!" her voice cut right through the cacophony, simultaneously leaping like wildfire into Beth's heart.

~

Her name was Kalliope but everyone called her Kay.

Probably just as well Beth hadn't known who she was—chairperson of the student's congress at their school and on the executive committee of the region—else she would never have spoken to her. Kay, at all of sixteen, already had a reputation. The story had become legend. A girl in Beth's class said Kay'd had an argument with Mr. Salie at the last Student, Parent, Teacher meeting, calling him a coward to his face. A parent had retorted.

"Show some bladdy respect for your principal."

"And when will you show respect?" Kay had shot back without a quiver in her voice. "Doing nothing while your countrymen get shot almost every day. But you go to church and ask to stay meek?" A glint of madness and danger had shone in her eyes, it was said, which the woman must have seen, because she sat down and said nothing else.

Kay's father was serving ten years on The Island for treason. Kay said he'd been arrested for trying to bomb a police station. This explained a lot to Beth. Like why Kay wore whatever she wanted, rejecting the go-to Struggle fashion trend of jeans, T-shirt with slogan, and Arafat scarf, opting instead for a decades-old style that no one—or at least no one not as brave as Kay—would be caught dead in. She was the real thing. A child of the revolution. A revolutionary in her own right.

16

After their first encounter, Beth wanted to see Kay again. But the next meeting was weeks away.

That Tuesday Beth saw Kay reading at the top of the stairs, refusing distractions or to give way to the march of school shoes. At least she wasn't surrounded by the comrades arguing passionately and smoking as they usually did behind the school. No way would Beth walk up to that group ever again. Beth rushed to the library hoping the book was in. After that, she climbed past Kay twice, who was still resident on the steps in an untidy mix of legs, lunchbox and bag. Immovable.

Finally, on her third rotation, Beth said, "Erm . . . Kay?"

"Ja. Beth, right? Been thinking about you . . . haven't seen you on the bus. Wanted to tell you about a meeting."

"Oh, ja, my father picked me up whole of last week. Old man was on leave. Heard the next meeting was two weeks away . . ."

"Those are the official meetings. We got unofficial too."

"OK . . . great, can do . . . so, you like to read?" Beth said, checking the spine of a pale pink volume that Kay was holding. "I was about to re-read this . . . here . . . from the library." Beth picked the book from her bag: *The Color Purple*, still new, with a tight thick plastic coat, checked out twice before.

Kay received the book with both hands. "You read this?"

"Ja. Maybe you'll like it . . . I mean if it's your thing. It's not politics-politics but it's not *not* politics . . ." Beth said, and shut her mouth so forcefully her teeth clattered.

"I love this book," Kay said so softly Beth had to move closer in.

"Oh . . . I thought cos no one had taken it out . . . been there for months."

"I took it out once."

"Then, I was the other time . . ."

"Thank you," Kay said, holding the book to her chest. "You know . . . maybe we can talk about books . . . I don't get a chance to read besides for politics-politics any more. Hardly anyone reads here. Bring me what you've read this year? We can talk when you come to the meetings? You're still ready to sacrifice your life for the Struggle, right?

Beth stared at her.

"Jokes, man. It'll be lotsafun."

Kay lived with her grandmother five minutes away from Beth in a part of Water Falls that no one walked through unless they were unlucky enough to live there, or they had a death wish. Why else would anyone be caught in the Skriwe Flats? The gangs gathered right there on the veld and battled, knife to axe to panga to Makarov pistol, whatever it took, because of some territorial discrepancy, or because one of theirs had been arrested on a tip-off, or because the sun had shone too brightly that day, waking them up in a Mandrax-fueled rage. A six-year-old boy had been shot while playing cars in his family's living room, the bullet exploding from the gun's mouth, bypassing ten to fifteen men, all of them packing multifarious kinds of contraband, clipped a tin roof, took a left and went through the window of the lounge, finding the boy's skull.

"Kak like that always happens," Kay said as the girls pretended to do their homework. "That's why we have to fight the system. We have to change it. And it's not just apartheid but capitalism that's at the root of this evil. When liberation comes, we'll give everyone houses, proper houses, and work, even the skollies. Clean up the Skriwe Flats, paint it, make parks for the children, make sure everyone can go to school and have free education. Especially girls and women."

They started to see each other every day, even though Kay was a year ahead. Kay's abrupt ways and quickness to confront usually meant other girls avoided her entirely. Beth brought books and small talk about what was happening in the rest of the school, while Kay took care of political education and carrying the world on her shoulders. It was an unequal union to be sure, but Beth didn't mind. Not yet, anyway. No, they hadn't known until after they'd met how much each needed the other to stand straight, finding strength in the number two.

In their world, which they decided was theirs to shape no matter what Principal Salie and the government said, there were no worries over getting knocked up (or for that matter beat up) at nineteen, or finding jobs as semi-permanent cashiers, or dreams of white weddings. No. Their conversations sparked currents that ran from here, now, and lit the future all the way.

Beth quickly realized that only Kay knew the things she wanted to know. Like how to get more than three books out of the library right under Mrs. Adams's portrait's stare. Or how to light a new cigarette from a stompie. How to argue dialectical materialism. How to kiss a boy. How to apply lessons learned from Communist China to South Africa. How to flick a Zippo lighter with one hand. How to lead a toyi-toyi so it actually sounded and looked like a battle cry. How to do a fish plait. How to erect a barrier of burning tires across the main road. How to get the stupid cool boys to listen to you without them looking down your top. How to write a rhyming couplet. How to apply lessons from Communist Russia to South Africa. How to get the nerds to care about the Struggle as much as about their books. How to make Salie lose his temper so he started swearing like a bergie. How to lead a group of students to a mass rally. How to stay out past midnight. How to get the teachers to leave you alone. How to shout Amandla! without sounding sturvy. How to down a shot. How to be a revolutionary.

⌐ uses a list format
- lumps a bunch of things
  in together
- but also places revolutionary
  stuff as everyday stuff

3

SHANGHAI

I saw my typist days later, reverse-walking through the public gardens across the road.

Usually as I readied for work in the morning, I'd watch the spectacle of dozens of retired Shanghainese striding backwards as they took their exercise en masse. Decades earlier Chairman Mao had insisted that body and mind receive equal attention, and he'd introduced a vigorous routine via two radio broadcasts each day, so people were expected to stop what they were doing and begin the dutiful task of calisthenics. From my window I watched a group perform tai chi in its extravagant slow motion. Some waltzed together on a strangely located band of asphalt, mostly women pairing off as a stereo blasted tinny-sounding Mozart into the early day. I spotted him then mid-moonwalk.

I dressed quickly before racing down the ten floors of my building, past the narrow girls at reception, then the guards and drivers—not one without a smoking sixth finger as they waited alongside glossy black sedans, drawing hard, exhaling, repeat. Dodging a stream of yellow taxis, I reached the other side of the road and entered the immense public gardens. On the left were hedges that had been coiffed and clipped in exquisite symmetry.

* words & meaning

A Parisian summer garden. To the right a row of Balinese statues: stony women beckoning from a rhombus of cool water.

I caught up with him just as he entered the maze back to front, swinging his arms and pacing into the unknown. I slowed down, straightened my skirt and called out, "I have that word."

He greeted me out of breath, neither stopping nor slowing, so I had to walk quickly alongside him as he retreated or advanced (I didn't know which).

"Melancholy: could that be the word you were looking for?" Since he'd come to my door two weeks earlier, I'd not heard him typing—I felt responsible—and offered the word by way of regret. What else? Was there actual curiosity about him? Worse, was I seeking friendship?

"Melancholy." He paused, rolling the word over his teeth. "I know this word, a little like music," he said. "But no, too long."

"What about depressed?"

"Isn't this a doctor's word?" he said, circling his temple with his fingers.

"Unhappy?"

"Too simple."

"Dejected? Miserable? Disconsolate?" I'd made a list and was running through them as we performed our ungainly dance, my tapering grey skirt threatening to rip or pull me to the ground.

"Will . . . think . . . about . . . words . . ." he said, between breaths, before he began a series of squats, exhaling loudly as he stood back up, squatted and repeated.

I spun on my heel, more ashamed than angry. What had I been thinking?

22

"Wait," he called when I'd almost reached the gate. "You drink tea?"

"I do," I said, holding on to the gate as I decided whether to capitulate or resist.

"Come, we take tea," he said, almost charmingly.

The teahouse was in a traditional style of building that was hard to find, most of them demolished by the thousands decades earlier when youthful bands of Red Guards tried to cleanse China of a culture they believed repressive—a style which had made a contemporary comeback in plastic and plaster rather than stone and marble.

We sat awkwardly, two strangers who didn't know each other's names.

"Beth." I stretched a hand across the low wooden table, its carved legs and clawed feet brushing against my own.

"Huang Zhao."

It was eight a.m. and I was going to be late for work. Facts that didn't dissuade our waitress, impossibly lithe in a traditional qipao dress, from performing the tea ceremony drama. The woman's hands fluttered over the table, sterilizing and warming the cups before she dropped dried leaves into each and then in a seamless circular motion poured lukewarm water, so soon our cups beckoned with pale green blossoms. I reached out, but Zhao's hand halted me in the lightest of ways.

"Tea must rest," he said. "You know why Chinese take tea?" he asked, waving his hand with a flourish.

"It is traditional, no?"

"Tsst," he flicked his tongue off his palate. "Tradition . . ." he said dismissively, passing me a cup. "Chinese take tea for respect, for family. Sometimes for discussing important matters. Even, sometimes, to give a apology."

I called the office to say I was going to be late.

~

I was a consul now, but had started in government decades earlier, soon after leaving university and applying for a job in communications with the presidency. It was a lower-order job that I'd hoped might one day lead to the real work of governance. And back then, pushing papers and occasionally getting to the meatier stuff of pre-reading speeches or glimpsing the president's head or heels as he was ushered past in a tight entourage seemed adequate.

Early into that hopeful career, I'd met Andrew: a young lawyer who could switch in a beat, sometimes maddeningly, between putting up a sweeping defence of worker's rights to slapstick humour. Though his desk was on a higher floor of our building, he managed to walk past me once or twice a day. Back then I'd been uninterested; more, consciously against the idea of an office romance, despite evidence of Andrew's charm and brilliance; his steady ethics. So much had happened and I no longer wanted, didn't need by then, to explain myself to anyone, least of all a workplace suitor.

Yet how quickly I saw that Andrew could be picked from the crowd. He wasn't like the guys I'd dated and certainly like none of my young (or old) colleagues in American sunnies and Italian brogues who insisted that I smile . . . just this once for me, come on man? There was no hint or spirit of the comments—ice-queen/frosty/frigid/bitch—which I heard after refusing them.

After months of ignoring Andrew's subtle attentions I found myself alone with him, everyone else on an extended Friday lunch. Listen, you seem really interesting and actually, you know, I like you . . . I have for some time, he said, failing to shove his hair away so I took the unguarded moment to look fully at him. And then, hours later, over a drink, his head resting in his palm: What mechanisms are ticking beneath the quiet surface, mmmh? Finally: I love this severe shirt-and-skirt combo you always wear, he said, pulling me closer by my waist, undoing any, all, reserve.

Even if it had been a ruse (it wasn't) I was smitten and relented: My seriousness and single-mindedness for your wit and that curl, I proposed. Done, he said.

In my career, excelling brought with it unwanted scrutiny and questions about my past. I preferred quiet diligence. Invisibility at the margins, Andrew said. Every few years I swapped roles, moving from communications to economic affairs to energy, settling finally in the diplomatic corps. A permanent mid-level civil servant.

When did it start? That creeping, unnerving corruption that seems immovable now? When did it start to settle in to our departments and, it seemed, onto everything in the country, like a layer of grease? Right under my watch?

After a while Andrew changed jobs. And soon after that he refused to represent or work with anyone in government, gravitating closer to groups that opposed the ruling party, soon serving only those who were not in the act of betraying the revolution, he said.

It was a cruel arithmetic: the more we fought about it as the years progressed, the greater the divide between us. The small house we'd bought together in a diverse mixed-income suburb slowly growing old, losing its shine and becoming more lopsided along with the country:

"When did the walls develop those cracks?"

"What cracks? Oh, yes."

"And the plants? Didn't we have a band of blue hydrangeas running behind the wall once?"

"Did we? Nothing but dust now."

And then quite suddenly we were immersed: the war within and without. Andrew joined a practice that was actively, litigiously, opposed to government.

"You know by sticking with this regime, *with them*, you're letting the people down, right?" he'd say, flippantly enough so it seemed that my work was a minor annoyance to him. In fact, it sank to the centre of our relationship. Andrew was unforgiving once we began to see friends swayed by the lure of personal wealth or power. When a colleague I'd known since the early days of our careers, on the same salary scale, stepped out of a new Land Rover and began alternating a rainbow collection of Ozwald Boateng suits, Andrew condemned the man to whomever would listen, while for me—yes, yes, I confess—it felt like a greater betrayal to turn on him. After all, we had once shared such an intimate dream as freedom (perhaps the most elemental dream of all). Weren't *we* the ones who had created this new country? So no, I said nothing to our seniors. The work was all I'd truly known, I said by way of an apology to Andrew. Anyway, how could anyone walk away from a past that had fused us all together, the heroic and the duplicitous, whatever their shortcomings?

"Corruption, not shortcomings," Andrew said, "and by the way these were the same comrades that kicked you to the curb?"

"You know the reasons . . . how it almost broke me. Anyway, all was forgiven . . ."

"You make it sound like family and not a political party."

"Maybe it is family . . ."

He always had the last word.

I was dragging the past around with me, placing it in the centre of our lives, in fact there was a third entity in our love which really when you thought about it, this presence, this ghost had affected, no, shaped and reshaped everything so why look anywhere but to the past for a solution but no, please don't answer that I mean just don't. Slam. ⌐ importance of the past

I never did.

But what did Andrew know? He was an inconsistent man, careless in certain ways but resolute in others. He lost things: his wallet and driver's license, twice each; he abandoned the Jewish faith into which he'd been born, misplaced pens and forgot appointments. He'd even lost his sense of humour. Yet when it came to people, he was exacting to a fault, accepting neither perceived weaknesses, nor moral incertitude, at least as he saw them.

~

With Zhao that Shanghai morning I went through the motions of the cultural training I'd received, thanking the waitress and Zhao, taking care to flatter him on his choice of teahouse.

"No need . . . I understand you Westerners think to compliment pleases the Chinese mind," he said, so I blushed at how he'd uprooted the platitudes and at his own ones too.

"I'm South African. Maybe we're both mistaken . . . but, really, this weather," I said, fanning away a frown as much as the heat.

He didn't reply immediately; silence didn't seem to perturb him, and only after a minute or more had passed did his voice start up again, in dark rich tones. I didn't understand the Mandarin but knew from the weight of the words, their cadences, that he was reciting poetry.

"You know Du Fu?" he asked, when he was done.

"I do not."

"Tsst." He shook his head. "This is for us like Shakespeare. I know also in English:

It is fine to go boating in the setting sun,
the light breeze is slow to raise ripples.
The bamboo is deep, with places that detain the guests,
four lotuses washed clean, the moment we enjoy the cool.
The young nobles flavor iced waters,
the fair women pull off lotus tendrils.
Then a patch of cloud grows black overhead—
the rain will surely hurry our poems' completion.

If there'd been momentary unease at his falling into poetry, or at his blunt observations, it drifted off and all that was left were fragile verses on that summer morning.

"Lovely. I imagine better still in Mandarin."

"Course! Chinese Tang poetry is very complex, difficult, every character very important, but only seven lines. Tone very crucial," he said.

Overhead, the city had awoken within its own wonder. A roof glinted, a cloud hooked on a spire, a sky-high pearl gleamed as a barge sounded below.

Zhao said, "Some of these buildings so ugly. That one: pineapple, that one crazy English lady hat, that one bottle opening . . ."

"Bottle opener . . ." I suggested.

"Bottle opening," he confirmed. And then, as if I had just mentioned it,

". . . Melancholy: this word sits inside my chest."

"Yes," I agreed.

4

CHINA

1958

When last I saw my mother the plum rain season was at its end. She stood at the door twisting a skirt that had washed to grey and waved me away with her free hand, all the while eyeing the distance that devoured me in fractions.

My village was dying or already dead: not just its people but every living thing. First the animals had gone. Then grain and rice. And when those were gone, the insects, followed by plants and grass. Soon after, the bark vanished from the trees.

And then there was nothing.

What had happened to absolutely everything, you ask? Well, it was eaten of course. Who by? Well, the people themselves!

But where are my manners? Allow me to give you a tour, so you can see what I once saw. The Chinese countryside in my home province is the most beautiful in all the world. Granite rocks turn to gold as the sun crosses over peaks pointing repeatedly to the heavens, while soft downy clouds wrap those mountains. But why trust me? You can see these images in almost any traditional Chinese painting. In my most beautiful province you will also find ancient villages built during the Ming and

Qing dynasties. Picture if you will the traditional Chinese village of your dreams (or from the movie that Chinese find boring, *Crouching Tiger, Hidden Dragon*) with its sloping-jutting roofs, a mountain for its back and a river for its mouth. Ancient residences dating back almost one thousand years. Pay attention to the latticework, the intricate carvings, archways, beams and columns. Step carefully on the black or pink cobblestones that line the many lanes that weave together this ancient village. They have been beneath the feet for so long.

Now, cast your eyes to the places that cannot be seen. Behind there . . . no further, deeper, darker: yes there. My village was stuck between others. Still today no one visits unless they are lost or compelled to visit family during the annual New Year's celebrations. No, my village was not the China of pictures and poems.

Our houses, made of stone and thatch, were located close enough to the wheat fields that one could roll out of bed and land feet first in muck, wasting not a moment by walking to work.

But see now. I ramble about the past like an old man, though my memory is filled with holes. At least I have the books I have kept all these years to fill the great gaping voids. It is not one book that I have used to record the days and years, you understand, but many. You might call it a diary but I never could. It is nothing so precious. My little black book (the joke's on me) was kept first so I might recount the events to my mother when she reappeared. Then, because I needed to recall them for myself.

I was away at school when I received news to come home quickly. Aunty, who had helped raise me and was sister to my beloved mother, was sick and would not live past the harvesting of the wheat. I dropped everything and left as soon as I could. Food by then was already scarce, but I took my ration of rice, begged for and borrowed more, so even the woman at the school canteen took pity and gave me extra.

It was 1958 then, one decade after the communists had taken control of China. The land that had once belonged to the wealthy landowners had been confiscated soon after the revolution, and first divided between us peasants in equal measure. But they had a change of heart (don't they always?) and decided they had better control all of it, so soon collectivization was instituted. Mind you, Mother's and Aunty's lives were better than they had ever been, there was food enough for everyone, they had their cherished son and they had been newly liberated from peasantry.

I reached our village after hours of travel. I approached our home after the long dusty walk, and my eyes fell on Aunty visible through the open doorway. If not yet dead, she was hardly alive. The jacinth skin which had once stretched across her flesh now drooped from her bones like badly sewn cloth. She looked at me with such sorrow, yet her body was so dehydrated, so starved of nourishment, that her eyes declined to tear.

Together Mother and I cooked congee. No matter, for it was all too late and Aunty died later that same day as we sat beside her, weeping for every day we had spent in her company and every lost day to come.

Mother promised that she would leave the very next day, after a decent meal of the rice I'd brought. She said she wanted to mourn before burying Aunty, and only then would she go to stay with family at the county seat, just on the other side of the mountain, where surely such a cruel and heartbreaking fate, such hunger—a famine for the ages—did not await her. She insisted that I should return to school immediately and assured me of her safety despite my reluctance to let her go alone. Why could I not wait and see that she was safe? Deliver her there myself? But no, she was adamant that she was still my mother, and I, as her child, must obey. She promised she would leave soon. In my grief I suppose I must have conceded.

~

Do my memories of old village life deceive me?

I swear on summer evenings after we'd eaten, bathed, and tidied up, we'd sit outside exchanging stories from the Qing dynasty with our neighbours. During the ripening of the plums everyone was in a festive mood, and we would admire the fruit trees and birdsong, all the while gossiping or listening carefully for news carried from the county seat, where the administrative and political offices were located.

During those golden evenings my mother and Aunty would spend hours arguing about who the better poet was: Li Bai or Du Fu, beloved since the eighth century and known to all Chinese from childhood. Aunty insisted it was Li Bai by virtue of him being the older, and so the true and original genius. But Mother never tolerated such talk. No, Du Fu never accepted his lot in life, he fought the corrupt and spoke his mind. Aunty would always tap Mother quietly on the leg when the conversation took such a turn. It was not the time for complaints of such a nature

34

unless one wanted to find oneself before a struggle session, guilty of rightist thinking. Everyone knew what happened at the dreaded sessions—it happened for all to see—those who strayed from the path of the revolution (or complained about the land that had been given to peasants only to be taken away again so soon) were brought before the crowds to be chastised, kicked, and often beaten, some dying for their inability to hold true to communist ideals.

I must scour this little book of mine to see evidence of what I thought; what I must have felt about the things that happened all around me. What my memory is in no doubt about is that I believed without question that disloyalty was not to be tolerated if it stood between us and our collective dream of freedom. China was undergoing a radical transformation from a humble agrarian economy to an industrialized nation. The Great Leap Forward. After one hundred years of imperialism we Chinese had felt, been, utterly downtrodden, but we were no longer on our knees. We rejoiced at the freedom the Communist Party had brought, giving us back ourselves. Not for a moment did I consider Aunty's death, and what I would soon understand to be my mother's disappearance, as anything more than personal tragedies brought on by that devastating famine.

Neither the little black book nor my memory disagrees on this fact: I believed, most solemnly, in the Chinese people and our national project.

5

SHANGHAI

I'd been in the city for three months when our regular walks began. I told myself we became friends by coincidence: bumped into each other on the stairwell, saw each other by chance in the garden, fell in step going the same way. Maybe this was more believable than the reality that we both needed someone to walk beside, to speak with about more than the price of a piece of fruit. It wasn't his charm. I suspected he'd say the same about me.

Anyway, the solitary walks had become too much. Too filled with thoughts about Andrew, how I'd left, what should happen next, my wondering what or who was to blame. Ideology? Places of work? Or that Andrew had simply met someone else and it was easier to blame me than be truthful. Finally, unable to sleep one night, I emailed him: "I left and you let me go. And I suppose, after that, what remained?" The honesty, accusation perhaps, aimed away from me, allowed some of the murk to begin to dissipate. At least it was a partial unburdening, one that permitted a look ahead, or, at least, elsewhere.

~

One Sunday, weeks after Zhao and I had tea, I saw him roaming the park across the road, head hung low. He saw me enter the garden, slowed, and with hardly any kind of greeting beckoned me over.

"I was just on my way out," I said. "I'm going to Xintiandi. Do you want to come along?"

"No," he said.

"Oh."

"Too many tourists drinking coffee."

"You don't like coffee?"

"Also tourists. Anyway, Xintiandi not really Shanghai."

"What?" I said. It was very much Shanghai. Every tourist brochure, every expat meet-up mentioned the old alleyways with some reverence as being exactly what the city had once looked like.

"Rubbish. Xintiandi. Disneyland. Same."

"Oh."

"Come," he said, brightening by degrees and offering to take me on a walk in an effort at my re-education. To pull the blinkers from my Western eyes, he said, or something like that beneath an elaborate grumble. We soon found ourselves walking down narrow lanes that I'd consciously, or worse, unconsciously avoided in all those months. He said I'd been too arrogant to truly understand the city, to walk into its heart, and I didn't say so, but feared that I had been too squeamish, put off by the city's mysterious odours, its dangling washing, its people sitting around evaluating us foreigners warily. Because I was no stranger to poor neighbourhoods hidden in a city's folds, I accepted his scolding.

From a narrow alleyway, deep in the shadows of the vertical city, we stepped through an arched opening in a huge stone wall and emerged into a courtyard. A handful of elderly people milled about in their summer pajamas, immersed in the ordinary drama of life: playing cards, talking and drinking tea among their collective detritus—bicycles, plastic wash basins, floor mops, a chair or two holding up, it seemed, all of Shanghai's unused things. A violin was being plucked somewhere in the background, the same notes over and over again. The old folk stopped momentarily to watch us. What a strange combination we must've made: a man of their generation who might have sat with them on any other day and a younger non-Chinese woman who was . . . well, what would they think of my ancient mash-up, courtesy of multiple continents? A hint of Asia around the eyes. The extra-thick hair in the ponytail, that mouth, that nose? Asian-African-European? Anyway, not Chinese (or maybe more generously: striking as Andrew had always said—never beautiful—oblivious of the sting).

"Shanghai," Zhao said.

Behind the group of people stood an elegant and ancient building, nature breaking through intermittently as pot plants and flowers in bloom.

Everyone went back to their business after cursory greetings. A woman washed vegetables at an open sink complaining, I think, to no one in particular about nothing especially troubling. A young woman, straddling a toddler trying to climb her legs or swing from her arms every few moments, hung washing as she laughed and sang a song in Mandarin to the tune of "Frere Jacques."

"Where are we?"

"Shikumen lilong: *proper* old neighbourhood, with Chinese and Western characteristic," he said. "Outside courtyard is Chinese, but house like in the West, no?"

They were narrow row houses, three floors high.

"The building with European influence, Chinese feng shui. And now, one family is on every floor. Maybe twenty families in here."

We walked further into the maze of little streets, curiously cut off from the clamour of the city just behind the thick stone wall, metres away. Zhao stopped every once in a while to point out something: a typically European column or gable, or an intricate Chinese wooden lattice embellishing a walkway that belonged to another era.

"Many Chinese families live here together and social together."

"Socialize together . . ."

"Yes, social together. See your neighbours when you cook. Talk any time of day. Many families with one heart."

"Why do you live in a compound with so many expats?" I asked. The rest of the city was a grid of apartment blocks, lining street after street with units stacked perpetually above the other, it seemed, and neighbours might not know each other at all, aside from the occasional meeting in a stairwell or elevator.

"Life like this kind, but sometimes busy. Cannot think, work."

I didn't have the courage to ask Zhao if that work included the typing I'd once heard, but no longer did, as we went on our way.

"Why weren't these demolished?" I asked, testing ground gingerly. I knew, and he never needed to say, that certain things

40

were out of bounds. Any talk of Chinese politics, for instance, or derogatory mention of Chairman Mao. This was simply how it was between most Chinese and foreigners, a veil hung between certain subjects: the 1989 massacre in Tiananmen Square, the Dalai Lama, Tibet. One didn't know where another stood, only that discussion would not be welcomed, was maybe forbidden for a Chinese citizen.

"Old Shikumen houses belonged to capitalists," he said, not ignoring my question entirely. "A rich man maybe built this for many sons but after the revolution, this become a home to many poor families."

Before we reached the main street, he took me by the arm and directed me into a little store I'd almost missed, its door roughly cut into heavy stone. It was dark and dank inside but when my eyes adjusted I saw thousands of books in various functional arrangements: keeping the doors ajar in the hope a breeze might waft in, holding an electric kettle, filling corners and lining every bit of space along the walls. It was cramped and dirty, yet took my breath away.

"Long ago many hundred print houses and book shops here, so revolutionaries could hide, meet secretly," he said.

"Before communism? You mean in the 1930s there were many bookstores on this street?" I gestured towards the row of hair and nail salons, video stores, restaurants, repair shops.

"Tsst. Yes, *before*."

"Langston Hughes wrote about these sorts of places, these alleyways. Maybe even this one."

"What?"

41

"I almost forgot," I said, digging around in my bag. "Those letters . . . you seemed interested when you came by my place a few months ago. I thought you might want to borrow it."

He accepted the slim book delicately, between thumb and forefinger.

"Langston Hughes wrote a bit about his stay in Shanghai in there."

Zhao paged through the book. "Letters to who?"

"I'm not entirely sure; no one is. He never addressed the person by name and all that was clear was that he was writing to someone in Cape Town."

"Why this secret?"

"I guess the times were dangerous. They were both dissidents, and letters might have been easily intercepted. But we know the correspondent was a writer; a man. Then again, the letters were donated anonymously to a university . . ."

He wedged the book into his armpit.

Careful, I wanted to say, but refrained.

"But these were the sorts of places he visited before the revolution," I said and waited, my silence a clear signal that I was ready to hear more about China's politics.

". . . We talk another day. Tired," he said, walking me back in the direction of the main street.

~

I can't say that the story I started to tell one evening as we strolled along the river was without forethought. After all, didn't I want to crack open Zhao's reserve? Broach the unsaid?

The massage parlour across from our apartment block changed its name, I began. Had he noticed? One day, as it had always been, it was called Gang Guo Tang, the meaning I think having to do with Chinese traditional medicine?

"Correct."

But overnight, a new sign had been erected. The previous one, also written in Pinyin— the system of writing Mandarin in the Roman alphabet—had been replaced by a flashing electronic sign with the words *R. Soul*. At first I'd stood staring at the new name, wondering what had become of my massage parlour, I told Zhao. I ventured in to find the receptionist seated at her usual spot. It was just a new name and she couldn't say how it had all come about, only that her wealthy Beijing boss had made arrangements for a team to change everything: the sign outside, business cards, and new slippers and uniforms that would arrive in days.

Only as I chatted with the receptionist did the full meaning of the new name become apparent to me. I covered my mouth, suppressing a rude laugh.

Zhao stared at me: "Explain R. Soul then?"

"I thought you'd know . . ."

"No . . ." he answered, wary, as he always was, of criticism.

"Zhao, well, I can't say more than that . . . but it is a very intimate part of the human body, and whoever advised the owner was probably mocking him."

"Part of a lady body?"

"Everyone has one."

"On face?"

"No."

"Upper part?" He was more obstinate than I'd imagined. "Front or back?" he continued, enjoying it as I blushed.

"No, you will have to ask someone, anyone else," I said, as he shook his head.

"Always you people point out bad English, never bad Chinese."

"I'm always apologetic that I don't speak Mandarin. But anyway, who do you mean by 'you people'?"

"Westerners."

"All of them are awful? Really?" I said into his shrug. "And would I have pointed out the cruelty of the name if I didn't care? I told the staff that they needed to let the owner know that the name was inappropriate."

"You laughed?"

"Come on . . . only a little. And I'm South African."

"More them than us."

"Neither *them* nor *you*."

"Not enough of China's friend."

"Well, then you haven't heard: South Africa is such close friends with China that we won't let the Dalai Lama visit." His face drew closed.

I knew I'd said the unsayable; had wanted to say just this.

"You don't see all the news . . ." I said, in a softer tone.

"Watch international news . . ."

"Edited," I said, referring to the delay in the newsfeed, occasional missing segments, the banned social media forums and websites.

He stopped walking and turned to look at me. "China does good work for Africa," he said, and I shook my head at this often-repeated phrase.

"Sometimes yes, but sometimes also not."

"Explain."

"China pursues business, builds needed infrastructure all over Africa: roads, train lines, bridges. But it's business, not humanitarianism. Look, yesterday I heard of an incident in a neighbouring African country. The workers went on strike because they were earning too little and said they'd not been properly trained or equipped; they were treated poorly, not provided with sufficient or quality food. In turn, the Chinese managers accused them of being too stupid to understand the complexities of the work. It wasn't the first time I'd heard such a story: Chinese managers behaving as if they were overlords, superiors, while the workers were little more than peasants. So no, Zhao, this is no favour but business as it has been for centuries." — look to the past

"Awful . . . all, really?" he hit back.

And then in his peculiar chivalry, saying nothing further, he gave a deep nod, almost a bow, turned and left, leaving me alone on the river bank.

By the following morning I regretted our fight. Despite being weary of the hackneyed narrative of China the hands-off partner offering to raise African countries up minus political interference, I was a diplomat, and my words were beyond hasty; they were irresponsible. More than this, I wondered what the price would be of my clear conscience, of speaking my mind.

Yet that Sunday there came a steady, slow thudding at my door before it had turned eight a.m.

"*Chi fan le ma*? We eat street food today," Zhao said, and paced the lounge as I got ready.

I'd always refused street food in what he said was typical Western arrogance. And so we walked until we found you bing, green-onion pancakes eaten with fried eggs. He bought a bowl of soupy spicy noodles and nudged me to have some, so I plunged in my chopsticks, and tried not to think about sharing food this way with anyone but Andrew.

We didn't speak about our disagreement; each time I tried he changed the subject until I said no more. But if there were a starting point to our friendship—a definitive moment when the thing became unmoored, when the artifice was stripped so we could begin honestly, become friends, perhaps it was then.

6

HARLEM

1953

Dear Friend,

It is early May and already it is hot as the dickens on the East Coast. Though I am not much encouraged to write when the air barely moves, answering letters is one of life's necessities and it was time to attend to yours. Thank you for the news from your hemisphere: Cape Town, man, you sure are far!

Now, you've asked a hundred questions of me: what I'm working on, what I do in my private time . . . several more! Let me begin at the most pressing of them all: how had I come, you asked, to be called to testify before the American people?

Seems I might do well to oblige you. For the sake of brevity let me begin in 1933, late July, when the sun was then too breathing heavy on my back.

I awoke in a strange room with this thought: It was not Harlem. Just because I had been dreaming of Harlem didn't mean it would materialize, even if I had been called the Poet Laureate.

I had been away from home for almost one year by then. I'd left New York City for Moscow the previous summer. The reason this poet became peripatetic? An invitation to appear in a film in Russia (the picture did not happen but that is another story). Still, I stayed a while, making a great deal of friends and travelling at times to the furthest outposts of the USSR. Every day I woke up curious to know how life worked in these foreign cold climes. Certainly, as a person of color outside of the USA I was especially interested in how I'd be received, but the mundane fascinated, too: the many varieties of food, languages, culture. The very humanness of humans!

After I'd been in the USSR almost a full year, I went on to visit Japan and China by way of home. And it was in Japan, to my delight, that I was warmly embraced as the first Negro poet to have visited! I guess back then it was considered strange for a Negro—maybe any American—to travel at all, never mind as far as the Far East. So my visit was often met with surprise (mine and theirs).

After more than a year of journeying my feet found the Asiatic metropolis of Shanghai. It is here where the story I must tell you takes place.

Would you believe that I had just begun to wander those strange streets when from my rickshaw I saw a man who looked to me like a fellow Harlemite? In China of all places! And in my excitement, I shouted from across the street:

Hey . . . hey, you there! My hand raised in greeting. But to which the fella was too stunned to reply.

I wanted to take his hand and ask how he found himself so far from home. What had brought him to Shanghai. But he passed me by and we never did see each other again.

No matter my thoughts of home because Shanghai was its very own thing: the many kinds of vessels jamming up the harbor from all corners of the world beneath a sun hot as the devil himself, and a sky so blue that the sea had seemed endless at first. Shanghai was on the cusp of a river, the Whangpoo, across from which was an untouched, flat expanse of land that stretched as far as the eye could see. Stark contrast to the other side's hullabaloo with its smartly designed buildings ranging from European banks to American missionaries. I walked the Bund (rhyme it with fund) and decided that perhaps I would pay no mind to the color lines that I'd been repeatedly warned about after all. How many times had I been told not to trust any Chinese outside of the international settlements and certainly never to go walking outside the barriers any time of the day or night?

The yellow man hates the black man more than the white man does! Slit your throat where you stand, sang the chorus.

It seemed to me it wasn't the Chinese who cared so much, given that I had to search for a hotel in Shanghai that did not practice its own kind of Jim Crow (no black, no Chinese and no dogs allowed!). Man, I was terrified of going into some of those smart European hotels!

The city's geometry then was a savage mix that fractured Shanghai into Russian, French, British, and American concessions. The Chinese kept out with razor wire.

I reckoned early that I'd be alright wherever I decided to go. And this is just what I did.

I decided to pay no mind to the stories about food either. In fact, on the morning that my story takes place, I had stopped at the concession stand outside my hotel and, hungry as wolves, bought from an elderly lady one, two, three plump white buns and a cup of fragrant tea. Delicious! And the watermelons that I'd been told were dragged along the length of the Yangtze River so they might soak up the filthy toxic water, growing fatter and rounder as they made their way to market? I bought a slice of the sweetest, reddest jewel-like melon I'd ever eaten. I did many times and I was just fine.

Well, what could I make of that multiracial city? I'd set up my Remington portable no. 2 typewriter (which by then had followed me from Harlem to Moscow, Tokyo and finally Shanghai) at a desk which overlooked a crowded street that housed a post office, a little store selling various things including tea and tobacco, and a host of vendors selling food so the whole malodorous cacophony reached me as I tried to work.

Shanghai in 1933 was a city that would not hold still. Any time of the day or night inside the international settlements or without if you knew which streets to go, or rather in my case which to avoid, one could find any kind of vice: crooked old ladies selling young girls or boys for an hour, whores from almost anywhere on God's planet—from Russia to France, Japan or England—while opium dens dotted the city, offering an escape for as long as a man might desire. If a body disappeared, well, no one might notice for a while. Death, it seemed to me, accompanied life a little too closely and I reckoned those to be some of the hardest streets I'd walked. Just earlier in the week two American missionaries, ladies who despised color lines everywhere, showed me round a factory where girls and boys as young as ten toiled for fifteen hours each day, given up by their parents in order to bring food to their families' tables. Most of them would not have survived that childhood. Even now, twenty years later, this memory grabs hold of me and doesn't let go.

Much as the tales of your own city unfold in your letters that I await eagerly, I've come to know that no place is either one thing or the other, and anyone could get lost in Shanghai's finest hour. If you had some money, or some reputation or perhaps some beauty—as many women and indeed men, too, had—then you might spend an evening in the private baths, or dance the night away in a jazz club to tunes made popular back home. There was no shortage of jazz clubs in Shanghai in 1933 and the place had a particular proclivity for African-American performers. I became friendly with some who were a fixture in the East, moving as they did from Singapore to Shanghai, summer to winter, all while entertaining foreigners and locals alike. Them fellows from back home with their Japanese, Russian and American wives and girlfriends showed me a grand time in that city. They lived life according to their own rules, ignoring color lines as they pleased (and many other conventions too) and amongst themselves were putting in place a world that perhaps one day we too might come to know.

By then Japan had already bombed parts of the city and was edging closer to a full invasion.

Between the odd smells and sounds rising off the sidewalks in Shanghai, I could get nothing done. I must have been in the city less than a week when I rose from my desk, grabbed my shoes and made my way into the day. I reckoned I would walk to the offices of a journalist whom it had been suggested I call upon. I had barely walked a block or two, waded it seemed to me through the hot muggy day, when I got the distinct impression that I was being watched. Why, every time I stopped to admire something in a shop window or have a look at an interesting detail on a building, a man just visible in my peripheral vision appeared to stop too.

I knew, had known for some time that the Chinese government of that day did not like writers, and two years shy of my visit, the anti-communist Kuomintang (who had helped liberate the Chinese from the Qing dynasty, leading to the establishment of a republic some twenty years earlier but now turned against their own) had murdered five writers. Can you imagine being hunted down over a manuscript? But then as your stories show, of course you can and I am sorry to say I watch with concern as your own government (or at least the one that rules South Africa) becomes more repressive each day.

I feel that I can state myself clearly with you, since you ask that I post these letters to different addresses all the time, under different aliases. Be assured that I am equally cautious as I too do not want my letters intercepted. The fear of a communistic system taking hold in China back then—of the 1930s—and today in my country (I am certain the stories of artists being exposed because of their political beliefs reach you, and I will tell you soon of my own predicament) drove men to irrational acts. I have never joined an organization, fearing that my independence would be compromised, and I would not call myself a communist (neither then, nor now), but I understood, indeed approved of the idea that the black and yellow and red men of the world might finally unite to throw off the long shadow of oppression, so I listened with some sympathy to the dreams of my Chinese brothers and sisters.

I digress: no, I was an American citizen and believed myself to be safe in Shanghai in 1933 despite what my fellow Chinese writers were experiencing and decided that I would not pay heed to paranoia. I took a left turn down an empty alleyway which snaked alongside stores selling a world of books. If anyone were following me this was sure to smoke him out. I bent down and made as if to tie my shoelace, and from the corner of my eye watched to see if anyone was behind me. I had not been there for even a moment, when I saw a man enter out of breath, searching for someone. Me? I rose hastily, quickened my step, and spotting an empty book store, I entered, pressed my body hard and flat against an interior wall and waited to see if he would pass. The stranger hurried past the store looking this way and that, before he spun gracefully on his heels and rushed off in the same direction in which he had come. So shaken was I by this incident that instead of returning to my hotel, as I might have done had I had my wits about me, I continued on my way to see the journalist that I'd set out to visit that strange day. I could have done with a friend and a strong shot of something but neither came to pass, for as soon as I reached the offices what I saw stunned me: every desk in the small office had been torn apart, every typewriter lay shattered on the ground amongst a field of blank papers. The offices had been utterly destroyed! Where were the journalists? Alive or dead? Who could have done such a thing?

I leave you (as the storyteller must) on a knife's edge as this bag won't be packing itself (I am delivering a speech next evening at Yale and I must prepare).

But before I go, one more matter: something must be said of my current situation, for news travels and you may come to hear of it. I am one of many who has caught the scrutinous eye of a certain Senator McCarthy. Should you hear about it, I ask that you read always with care and an open mind. It is a worrying time for artists everywhere, but I take much comfort in this anthology that brings me short stories, articles and poems from across Africa. After all, I would not have come to know the fine talent at the tip of that grand continent, to whom I address this letter, had I not undertaken the important job of introducing African writing to America.

But now, dawn is breaking and a rooster has just crowed (or perhaps it is just Ol' Man Johnson next door exercising his throat, as he does), and so my friend I will resume my writing (and my telling) once again soon as I can.

Yours sincerely
Langston

7

CAPE TOWN

1989

As far as Beth was concerned, the whole of Water Falls was an accident stuck behind the mountain. Happenstance, chance, apartheid and all of that had conspired, and there they were pretending at life with their colour televisions and couches on hire purchase, praying three hours every Sunday, all the while cursing the fine brown sand that made a mess of everything on a blustery afternoon. If her parents and the people they knew weren't so intent on their little comforts they might revolt, or at least get the fok out of Water Falls and relocate to the white sandy beaches where the ocean licked your toes and the mountain shielded your back from that persistently rude wind; places off limits to their kind.

Kay didn't like that sort of talk. Said it was disloyal to the working class, people like her, she said, who had no choice but to be in Water Falls and did the best they could. Which was what Beth meant anyway. Although she said nothing when Kay said they should always return out of loyalty. Beth didn't know about that. Even though she lived in a standalone in the nice half of Water Falls, it wasn't like they'd chosen it. Someone had drawn a map, designated people to place based on skin, and dumped them there. Beth reckoned that life, imagination itself, had stalled *there* where choice was freely given and shone like the aurora borealis *for them*. Anyway, it wasn't the working class that bothered Beth, it was the unemployed class that got to her: the way the women walked around in gaudy hair rollers and housecoats, getting beautiful for what exactly, while the men knew better and just sat around in their vests drinking papsak wine all day and smushing their wet lips together to whistle after girls too decent to look their way. Kay said that was a simplistic analysis, that race and class had conspired to make people, men especially, victims of the system, to emasculate them, thus rendering them powerless to effect their own change.

~

The girls passed a group of men sitting outside playing klawejas on an old upturned drum, the smell of dagga and burning rubber so thick in the air they instinctively held their breath. Or perhaps it was out of fear. They had just left Kay's place, and even though it was early afternoon, the Skriwe Flats wore a special brand of menace on payday Friday.

"Mornings ladies . . . where yous going on such a nice day? Come sit here with us . . ." someone from the group called. Kay stopped and caught the eye of the offender.

"Hey, Sammy Jacobs, why you still sitting around at two p.m.? My granny said the toilet is leaking again there by your mother them. She said yous must fix it before she come do it herself . . . stinks to high heaven," Kay shouted back. How she spoke was dependent on the source of her attention, and apparently Sammy Jacobs deserved this.

"A weh . . ." the group of men started to laugh and Sammy swore beneath his breath and pointed a finger at Kay.

"Kay, should you do stuff like that?" Beth asked, hooking her arm into her friend's and dragging her away as fast as she could.

"Man, I know Sammy, known him since he was a lightie. He's just playing at being a skollie. He's kak smart, came first in school. Coulda become a doctor if they had the money to send him to varsity or if he didn't get high when he was supposed to be looking for a scholarship. But his family got plenty problems. Now Sammy sits smoking pills and playing cards all day."

There were no meetings, or lessons or exams to dominate that Friday, so instead the girls were on their way to the beach. They jumped the train all the way, moving from one car to the next via the inter-leading doors as the train sped at two hundred kilometres an hour through the suburbs, the girls expertly on the run from the train gaajie who would fine them if he caught them without tickets, before depositing them midway along their journey. But he never could catch them.

Somehow between the wind that carried fine white sand into their hair and clothes, and the soporific sound of the ocean, the girls were infinitely distracted and neglected to even look at the pamphlets (all banned according to Kay) in their backpacks. Kay reached for her Walkman. She got fancy things from her mother, who lived in Johannesburg while Kay remained with her grandmother, where she was safe. One parent in Johannesburg and one in prison, said Kay, and their guilt could get her the moon if she wanted it. But she didn't want that.

Purple Rain was set to repeat inside her headphones.

"Hey Beth," Kay elbowed her, ". . . you know I won't live to twenty, right?" Kay said, between spurts of writing the lyrics into her diary, rewinding every few seconds so she could get them all. Ever since the girls had first heard him, they'd been devoted Prince fans, listening to few others, even though the comrades complained that they should only listen local or to Bob Marley. Still, the lyrics made Kay morbid, even a little unhinged.

"How you mean now?"

"I'mma die young. Always known it."

"Well, *that's* helluva pessimistic," Beth said evenly, though the coldness, the casualness with which Kay approached the thought of death, left her discomfited.

"Some people don't make fifty. Not even twenty. How it is."

"But what will be the point of anything, the revolution, if you're not there?" Beth said.

"Man, I'd mos die for your freedom," Kay said without skipping a beat.

In the heady days when they'd only just found each other, it astonished them how a friendship could weave a spell so tight, nothing remained of their previous lives. At least, that was how Beth felt, who brought books from the modest shelf her father—a diligent office clerk—had been collecting, borrowing and seldom returning, over a lifetime. Nothing political, but enough to build a mind, he said. He said no one could take away the knowledge you got from books.

Kay showed Beth the invisible world right beneath her own. You weren't supposed to say it, it was profane to think it, but it was a mad rush being in the Struggle. Hopping trains or riding buses, taxis, or a phalanx of these to suburbs and townships that Beth was not even supposed to know about. She saw the unimaginable when she went door to door pamphleteering: places so poor, so broken, they made an oil painting out of the Skriwe Flats. There was always room to go one floor closer to hell in this city. It made Beth's parents look like the comfortable sellouts they were. Since the Sunday that Kay had been invited for lunch, Beth had started seeing the world differently.

Beth's parents had insisted on meeting her new friend. They'd sat at the dining table before a grey blur of fish with potatoes. Neither parent had said much, which to Beth's mind had been the problem. When Kay took a potato from the dish with her bare hand, the quiet conversation that her parents had been having with each other stopped. Kay's voice grew louder, rougher with every syllable while Beth's mom blinked increasingly rapidly. Beth had never before heard Kay slurp, yet her drinking was so amplified, so oceanic, that her father sank a little deeper into his chair with every sip the girl took.

"Joh. Your parents are like what, Anglicans?" Kay had said as the girls walked back to her place.

"Anglophiles."

"Don't they laugh? Think they shit ice cream. And then not even chocolate. Vanilla."

Beth said nothing.

"Your parents don't like the way things are because it keeps them out. They want to be seen and heard, but don't want that for everyone. Definitely not me."

"S'pose so," Beth said, more saddened than humiliated, because she happened to agree.

"Why no laughter? It's the opposite at my place."

"Your granny the Maoist?"

"Ja. But she's only really a Maoist from Monday to Friday. Saturday she visits friends and Sunday she goes to church with her sisters, and afterwards they come over for a meal. They laugh, eat, sing, dance."

"On a Sunday?"

"Every Sunday of the year, man."

"There's no life in our home," Beth said.

"Too much in mine," Kay said.

Beth watched carefully from then on how her parents swanned around the neighbourhood feeling better than the people from the Skriwe Flats. Yet how her mother changed her accent, picked at her carefully done hair, or pursed her perfectly painted lips when they went into the nice shops, all so white ladies in pretty frocks could pretend not to see her. Or the soft tone her father used, his voice a sudden muted weapon, when a cop stopped him on the road. Beth saw it all. And capitulation felt like a lie. Complicity, Kay said, who had no time for games.

Mass rallies were electric. Police helicopters hovered. Tires smoked and hundreds of bodies toyi-toyied while the wild brilliant boys shouted from beneath their checked scarves, part disguise, part Struggle fashion trend.

iAtholone headquarter man, they called.

Sabotage!

iMitchellsplain headquarter man:

Sabotage . . . Qwaa qwa

They kept one eye trained on the cameras as they shot off air guns, the other watching if the boere would make a move and come running with their rubber sjamboks that thwacked the air, or worse, tins of teargas and R1 rifles.

When the police stayed at bay, watching only from a distance, a joyousness that Beth had never before known overtook everything. To know who you were and what you stood for, well, Beth had never felt that kind of freedom.

"Tch!" Kay said, "We doing this cos we *not free*, Beth." Even so, she smiled and Beth knew they were kindred.

It was only the Special Branch that gave Beth sleepless nights or worse, days interrupted by thoughts of prison and torture. They had files on everyone, probably even Beth by now despite her being low-key and more of Kay's sidekick than anything else. Kay on the other hand was on the executive student body of the region and her file must be brick-high.

"But what if the cops stop just hovering around school, and your home, and actually, you know, come arrest you, Kay?"

"Nah, they won't."

"How can you be so sure?"

"Told you already. One good thing about my father being a high-profile political prisoner means they don't want to arrest the child too. They get enough heat from international governments. Last thing they want is a headline saying *Struggle Hero's Child in the Mang.*"

If Beth had only listened to Kay, she might well have believed everything she heard. But Beth had come to recognize the sudden glances away, the quick flittering of Kay's eyelashes whenever she spoke about her father or mother, or the drawn-out silences after she said she didn't really miss them. Beth knew that Kay's words were to be weighed, stripped of their sheen, and read between lines.

~

Beth's attention drifted across the sand, ten, twenty meters to Surfer's Corner until her eyes found him. Mo Rasdien, his six-pack dispersing droplets of water as he walked out of the ocean, carrying his surfboard on his shoulder, wetsuit rolled low on his hips.

"Jassus."

"What?" said Kay.

"Brick. Shit. House," Beth said. "You think he notices us sitting here?"

"Too into himself, you can see that from a mile away."

"Do you think he exercises to get his stomach like that, or it just comes?"

"Two hours a day pumping iron, minimum," Kay said, as she lifted her head slightly from where it was lodged against her school bag.

"You think he likes girls like us?"

"What's that s'posed to mean?"

"You know: Struggle girls."

"Nah. He likes them pretty and stupid with hair that blows in the wind, not hair that gets stuck mid-air like this kroes kop of mine." She laughed uproariously and cupped her palms, lighting a cigarette in the wind.

"You think it'll always be like that?"

"Fok em. Can't change what you are, what you were given," she said, taking a deep drag. "No sense trying. Look at me—bushy head, fat lips . . ."

". . . Full lips, that's what the magazines say."

"I like that . . . ever see anyone ignore me? Don't give them the chance. Fok em. Once you start, it'll always be a moving target: straightener, skin whitener, slimming pills. One day people won't worry about stupid stuff like that," she said, starting to pack her bag.

Beth had stopped wondering about the mysterious meetings Kay had started attending recently. Or at least, so she pretended. Kay wouldn't tell Beth who she met, only that he was at university, it was a security risk for Beth to know any more and that she was learning things her friend wasn't yet ready to know. There was a Struggle hierarchy and Beth was a bottom feeder; a vantage from which she could at least surveil and learn.

"Come. Need to catch the five-thirty p.m. You coming or what?"

"Ja, in a minute," Beth said, shaking off the sand as she watched Kay make her way towards the station, so Beth was left momentarily to wonder what the meetings were really about, where Kay went, and how dangerous whatever she was up to was for them both. Also: how exactly did Mo Rasdien get his hair to fall that way.

8

SHANGHAI

Zhao's secrets revealed themselves by degrees. It was on the Sunday that we went in search of the magazine seller that I began to glimpse only some of what was being hidden.

We walked the length of Weifang Xi Lu looking for the man that sold an array of international magazines, in high demand by expats.

Zhao carried a smoke and an Americano, a new habit for which I was to be blamed, having introduced him to the pleasures of filtered coffee and the rousing din of the coffee shops that multiplied each day on the streets of Pudong, pushing against teahouses and, it seemed to me, a great deal more. Coffees in hand, we walked cement sidewalks, along roads which did not yield to pedestrians no matter their story: walking stick? Mother with a child strapped to her chest? Lost and alone dog? *Bu!* You can't cross here or anywhere!

We dodged cars to weave between fruit sellers laden with boxes of cherries, achingly sweet miniature mangoes, and fruits like sea anemones: yangmei, mangosteen, dragon fruit, and durian, which Zhao warned against, given their stink.

"Reading the book," he began, as we strode the sidewalk.

"The Langston letters?"

"Tsst. Of course Langston letters . . ."

"And?"

"What?"

"What do you think he was doing in China?"

"Who?"

"Langston, Zhao. Langston Hughes. He got into trouble for his visits here."

"Shanghai is very beautiful."

"Sure, I agree, but they thought he might have been a spy."

"Writer, spy; the same thing."

"Yes, but a spy spy. And this was serious. He chose a strange time to visit, no? Back then, in the 1930s, the communists were plotting the revolution and he came in the middle of it all."

"Tsst. Writers always making trouble," he said, cutting me off and pulling me towards the magazine seller, whom he'd spotted. The man was worth chasing, because he undercut store prices by half and had a wider variety: *Newsweek*, French *Vogue*, *Vanity Fair*—I had even found a *Barcelona Review* once. He had no fixed spot from which to sell his magazines and was liable to set up his wares wherever a fair spread of English readers congregated. Zhao joined me as I pored over the magazines spread on a canvas sheet, metres from the bakery which sold a variety of plaited breads and moulded striated cakes, with a shelf reserved for that strange taste sensation, the salty-sweet bun with its confetti of dried pork shavings. Zhao was looking at something from Hong Kong when a couple arrived. They were a study in androgynous beauty in their pastel shirts, matching white trousers, and alabaster skins, a faint scent of sunblock and their wide umbrellas sealing them off from the clamour of the streets. They chose a few English and Chinese magazines each, haggled abrasively, threw notes to the ground, and then walked away laughing.

"What just happened?" I said.

"Shanghainese . . ." Zhao said, by way of explanation. The city's native inhabitants spoke a language that was hard to penetrate, even for Chinese. Everyone said they behaved as if they owned the city. Perhaps they did.

"Flawless skins," I said softly. I'd been surprised at first at the many perfect complexions and quickly learned that in China, international beauty houses offered "White Forever" or "Bright White" so consumers were assured of agelessness as well as bleached skin. Back home, the same global companies weren't nearly as brazen.

"Say, Zhao, what do your people think of my brown-beige skin?" I nudged him, knowing he had started taking less offense at my questions.

But Zhao was transfixed by the magazine seller. I called him again. He looked at me but quickly returned his gaze to the man. His paper coffee cup had tilted, leaking hot coffee onto his wrist, so a layer of steam rose from his sleeve. I noticed a tremor in his hand and instinctively reached for it.

"Are you all right?" I didn't think of Zhao as old, but it struck me then that he was only a decade younger than my parents might have been if they'd been alive still.

"Let us go," he said, suddenly breaking away and walking off, his coffee sloshing out of its beaker and drenching a magazine, so the man started to shout. I pressed a hundred yuan note, three times the price, into his hands and hurried to catch up.

"What's wrong? Zhao? Perhaps we should sit," I said, looking around.

Instead, he strode ahead so I had to race to catch up as he discarded his coffee. He was headed towards the river. Only when we were seated on our usual bench did he resume the conversation.

"What just happened?"

"I know this man."

"Where from?"

"History."

"Was he someone famous?"

"No, in-famous?"

"Infamous? Why?"

"Forty years ago he murdered."

"Zhao, he only looks like fiftysomething now," I said, and placed my hand on Zhao's arm, to settle him as much as myself.

"He was age fourteen or fifteen then."

"*What*? But who did he kill? Why?"

"All of them."

"Who?"

"Children . . . so many died," he said and stopped.

"Zhao, I don't understand what you're saying."

"Chinese don't speak about this. We try to forget, but sometimes you see something, someone, and back to forty years before."

"The Red Guards?" I said, uttering the forbidden, and Zhao dipped his head and would be drawn no further.

He said instead: "For many, Chinese beauty and white skin is one thing," he said, definitively changing the subject. "This truth many will not tell. We even say: one white covers three uglinesses . . . I don't know," Zhao said, "maybe this from Han China, where women of court had white-milk faces. Poor women working in fields very dark, like my mother. Anyway, you are my people, so no matter."

I slipped my arm through his on hearing this, and held tight. Of course I knew about the Chinese obsession with fair flawless faces. Even so, Zhao's words astounded me, found a wound within, and pressed hard. I knew that the indistinctness of my beige colouring placed me outside the immediate circle of suspicion and loathing reserved on more continents than this for the blackness of my fellow Africans. But I didn't relax at being given a pass; I rejected it instinctively. It was a second impulse for people of colour, this: sensors on the skin or on the iris of the eye, always tracking what was being received, thought, emitted back to you at the moment. Felt most keenly in hotel receptions on arrival, airport customs in every new city, upmarket clothing stores. Quick glances—what did they think of you, the tone of your skin? And it would be no different here.

As we resumed our walk, I wondered what Zhao had seen and about his own hurts, why he evaded norms that others might not care to defy. I imagined too what the lovelies with their carefully protected skins would think about the men who held down street corners in Johannesburg, their blackness beneath a fierce sun, matted hair, feet and bodies covered in layers of poverty and neglect.

"Isn't this what Chairman Mao tried to rid China of, this sort of bigotry, during the Cultural Revolution? To stamp out old harmful traditions? The very kind of thing that gave rise to the Red Guards?" I asked.

We passed a billboard, a young European girl advertising cosmetics or a sweater, I couldn't be sure, her huge eyes and blank stare following us so we lapsed into a hollow silence.

"Talk tomorrow," he said.

I knew tomorrow would not come.

9

CHINA

1958 to 1962

By the time the winter months arrived, I was desperate for news. I had heard nothing, even the letters I'd written frantically to family in the county seat had gone unanswered. My exams were complete and it had been determined by the school that I would begin university soon.

Early one morning after I'd listened to the radio broadcast and we had all taken group exercise as the Chairman advised, I packed just a few things: a change of clothes, everything I possessed anyway, as well as a few books—my little black one, another for schoolwork, and a book of poetry. I took with me a ration of cooked rice that I had saved from the previous evening's meal. With the little money I had kept safe, I bought a bus ticket.

I thought only of Mother, my beloved, as the bus pulled away: what she would say to my worry and how she might chide me for not focusing on my studies. Why are you worried about an old woman when you know I can look after myself, she might say beneath a smile—in reality pleased that I was still concerned about her. It never fails to surprise me that at the time of her disappearance she was thirty years old; half my age today.

Soon she would drop the performance, admitting how much she'd missed me and perhaps she'd recite a poem by Du Fu so we would sit and laugh as we used to, crying occasionally for Aunty.

For many years after that bus trip I would tell myself that grief had clouded my view, for how else could I explain what I saw when I awoke hours later, nearing the county seat. The harvest had passed but as in my own village, trees had been stripped of their bark, the sky was plucked clean of birds, no mangy dogs scoured the streets, bereft of even a single mouse. I heard no children's voices as they chased one another on their way home from school, nor did I see men and women at work in the fields. My eyes entirely missed the elderly playing mah-jongg, talking the rich, lurid gossip of retirement. Only empty chairs guarded empty doorways. It was a ghost town.

I reached the house of Mother's cousin. He was an important man, a Party official and from what I could tell, as his wife welcomed me into their house, prosperous. No, she had neither seen nor heard from my mother, she said, but from what she understood our village had been all but decimated by the worst famine in memory.

For such a calamitous natural disaster to befall China so soon after our liberation could only make us stronger, she said. No, everyone had lost family members, sometimes an entire family had been wiped out, and my village, she thought, by now had ceased to exist. Cousin's wife said she couldn't think where Mother had gone and why they were suddenly not good enough to even tell about her plans. She must have seen the horror in my eyes because at once she changed the subject. You must stay for dinner, she said instead, and off she went to call someone to cook.

Did you not suffer a famine, Cousin, I asked, my voice trying to find itself.

But of course not. Why would you ask? she said, buzzing from one place to the next.

The trees, I said, it looks like the bark's been eaten, I began, but did not have the strength to continue.

A few people were hungry but that was because of rightist deviation. Anyway, it is important for all of us, even when hungry, to go through *the five mountain passes*, and she lifted a hand in demonstration: the revolutionary must view family, profession, love, lifestyle and manual labour—she flicked a point off each finger—with new eyes; give up privilege for the conscious acceptance of hardship and sacrifice. This is the only way that the great nation of China will advance.

You see, she said, the old landlords were hiding and storing the grain instead of handing it over. So many had to sacrifice while others, capitalists, hid food, she said, now polishing a little cup so studiously that I thought it might crack.

Surely in the villages, though, everyone had food, I asked? Cooking in private homes had been forbidden, replaced by communal kitchens meant to feed an entire farming community or village.

Correct, she said, the communal kitchen is an important unit in our nation for our advancement . . . so efficient.

I wondered if this must not have applied to Cousin and his wife, for at that exact moment I could smell food being cooked in the house.

By the time we were ready to sit down, chicken with peanuts and chilies, fish in broth, and many kinds of vegetables and dumplings had been prepared. I wrote it all down in my little black book and even scribbled down the side, here in the margin, a recipe Cousin's wife must have given me. My devotion was intense, I can see from how I doodled the Chinese flag on the page with precision, seriousness—over here a broken nib on the fourth star from the intensity with which I held my pen. I had committed to the Party, to Chairman Mao and our great revolution.

I hadn't seen such a feast since I'd left home to go to school; perhaps I'd never seen an opulent meal before. I ate ravenously—sucking, wrestling, ripping—so Cousin laughed when he came in and found me devouring the food.

Cousin was plump and handsome in his khaki Mao suit. We have been expecting you, he said. Still, he insisted they'd not received my letters.

I heard from your mother just after her sister died, he said, as he ate.

Then you did see her, Cousin, I said, trying to be neither disagreeable nor disrespectful, but I was desperate and could not understand why their story would not hold still.

I paid her village a visit on Party business some time ago. She was well, not too thin really, and though things had started to improve there, she said the memories were too much, and she'd seek work elsewhere.

She didn't say where she would go, Cousin, and didn't ask to come here?

Motherfucker, Cousin swore loudly, as he bit into a hard bit of the dumpling, and before I had time to look up, he'd flung the bun across the room, catching his wife in the mouth, so she yelped and disappeared around a corner. I invited her here, he continued unabated, but she insisted that it would not be right to use family associations to advance. She was good to know that sort of thing, he said, all the while stuffing food into the hole in his face.

I am sure one of these days she will send you a letter, for now you must eat bitter.

And the people who have starved, Cousin?

Surely you know, this is about the struggle between the two paths, capitalism and socialism, and it is the landlords and the capitalists, motherfucking pigs, that store and hide grain every place between here and the river, he pointed east, and here and the mountain, he pointed west, growing more animated, between land and sky, he stabbed at the ceiling with his chopsticks. They report falsely on what has been collected, to keep some for themselves, and this is why others have to give more and go hungry. The people starve because of the motherfucking pig capitalists. We must not for even one minute tolerate this. We must subject them to struggle, motherfuckers, we must tear them limb from limb. He wiped his mouth gingerly with a cloth, smiled and invited me to take tea.

I noted in my book that I was not asked to stay the night.

From there it was a short trip to my old village, and that is where I tried to go. But soldiers now patrolled the streets and we were not permitted to stop. Still, as the bus paused at a roadblock,

I stuck my head out of the window on seeing an old man from our village.

Farmer Lu, have you seen my mother, I shouted, but the man stared at me blankly. I called to him again, giving him my family name, for he had known my grandparents and indeed my mother since childhood. A creeping recognition seemed to dawn on him, but no, he shook his head, no, he did not know anything. Only that she, like so many, was long gone, he said, before he was ushered roughly away by a soldier. The engine started up then, the soldiers shouting for the bus to move on. After that, I would not see my home village for many decades.

10

CAPE TOWN

1989

It was harder to erect a burning barrier of tyres across the main road of Water Falls than it first seemed. Beth quickly learned that there were things to consider, like where to find old tyres in the first place and how many of these were enough? What flammable material should be used: dry sticks or newspaper, after all this wasn't a braai, and did you add these to the middle of the tyre or to the top? Would you use lighter fluid like a sturvy from the suburbs, or paraffin like a township comrade, and how did you stop the latter from drenching your arm so the orange incandescence would not race up your sleeve as screaming comrades tried to beat out the fire with their hands and their clothes until finally not a second too soon grabbed fists full of sand to extinguish the flame, but no matter because you still landed up in hospital before a long stretch of detention like Bongani from Langa township had discovered. Two years later he still walked with his burned arm nestled in his good hand and never wore T-shirts.

Most importantly, what the fok did you do if you had actually been ingenious enough to figure all that out with a ragtag team of wannabe revolutionaries of which you were bizarrely the most knowledgeable, had endured no personal harm, were well on your way to your first burning barricade so the mesmerizing flame was toyi-toyiing a metre from your nose, when you heard the not-too-distant sound of a police van speeding in your direction? Kay'd said to give the cops an hour, but they'd got there in a quarter of that. Well, Beth knew, you got the fok away as fast as your legs, themselves now leaping like fire from the location of your first crime, could take you, bounding over the six-foot wall that separated the road from someone's house, scurrying along the fence as you carefully negotiated around the freelance pavement special whose barks and teeth were cutting up the night air even closer to you than the flames had been, then dodging shouts of angry residents, "Voetsek! We don't want your Struggle here!" before you ran down a side road, another and another until fifteen minutes later, you stopped and realized your comrades had scattered in different directions, leaving you quite alone at night in the middle of the Skriwe Flats. If there had been a contingency plan, Beth had forgotten it entirely.

Beth did not know where she was or in which direction home was, only that it could not be very far. Still, it would be better to turn back, risking arrest, torture, and a potential jail term (as Bongani had) instead of the unlimited opportunities of hell that the Skriwe Flats offered.

She started down an infinite road, pretending not to see the men who stood cupped in the glow of neon street lighting—at least the globes that hadn't been knocked out by stones—as they started to raise their heads slowly in her direction. One set of eyes, another, then another, until the group was staring intently at the thin slip-of-nothing girl walking alone in a black-hooded top.

Inside her fear was a complex set of other feelings. Everything she had ever been taught screamed that the act that she had just committed was wrong. And yet, why did she feel like it had somehow freed her of a burden? Was allowing her to climb out of her old skin?

Since she and Kay had become tight, she'd given up plenty: old friends who couldn't stand her new politics or for that matter Kay, the mind-numbing pleasure of watching American soapies, reading nasty romances and listening to the wrong kind of music. Now her days were filled with meetings and minutes, appropriate books and music, and the occasional act of war. Plus, Kay said the movement had rules for days which Beth accepted because the way she saw it, when it came down to it, freedom was no choice.

Even the paralyzing terror that her current predicament would have resulted in weeks ago wasn't insurmountable. Something that could not be named was propelling her forward. Away from her old hopelessness, and her parents. She'd even handled the burning tyres project mostly alone, because of course Kay had disappeared again. Where the fok was she exactly? The barricade had been her idea.

"But why?" Beth had asked the week before.

"So people will see that the revolution is here, in Water Falls, disrupting the status quo, disrupting the neat comfort of their lives."

"But violence in our own neighbourhood, Kay?"

"Beth man, don't be dof. You can't have the townships permanently on fire, people dying but here in Water Falls no one gets involved cos they think coloureds are a class above. We got the same blood running in our veins; doesn't matter brown or black, we hated all the same. So dislodge their fear and make them understand that change is the only option. The sooner they get that, the quicker *they* will push for change. We not going anywhere. How do they see that? Every week there must be a burning barricade or a mass rally or pamphleteering. As soon as one thing ends, another must begin. There are some comrades planning something next week. You'll join up with them," she'd said.

Tactically, Kay abided by a certain code. The event or target had to make sense, and avoid harming people. She seemed to consult with shadow advisors before anything was decided. And yet why did she have to go and disappear a day before Operation Flame was to take place, leaving things to Beth and a few mismatched comrades? She was vanishing more often and for longer periods of time.

"Jou ma se poes. Jou pa se blou gat. Fok. Fok." Words that Beth had never before dreamed of saying and which came with greater ease than she could have known, sliced the air as she walked down that road, fear and rage burning her up from within. (Had it always been there?)

She could feel the lamppost men's stares impaling her, violating her every move. She would have started to run, she would have, had someone not crossed into her path.

"A weh . . . what you making here?" A woollen head with stubs. "I mos know you," the voice said, as hands were suddenly

80

released from deep jean pockets, a knitted cap was shoved away and eyes emerged to peer closer. "Are you jas to be walking here in the middle of the night?"

It was Sammy Jacobs, Kay's next-door neighbour.

"I was just leaving Kay's place, I'm her friend, Beth," she said, hoping that this civility would stop him from whatever he was about to do. She'd read that you had to make a personal connection. Say your name. Maintain eye contact.

"Talk kak. You one of the rioters burning up The Falls," he said, jerking his head towards the smoke that billowed high above the flats, so Beth felt equally ashamed and proud of the lurking black dragon. "Why yous come to burn tires here but yous live in the fancy houses?"

Beth tried to reply but the cold must have frozen her vocal cords.

"Come," he said instead, and began walking alongside her. "You live in Olivia Close." A statement. They walked down one road after the other (she was further from home than she'd known) him taking the lead, so when a group of men crossed their path, all he needed was to say a word, show his face, and the men were subsumed once again by shadows.

Only when Beth had been delivered unharmed to her front gate and she heard Sammy Jacobs's retreating footsteps did she realize that she'd not said another word.

~

The following week, Kay's grandmother reported that a yellow patrol van had started to pause each afternoon outside her

81

maisonette, idling there for a few moments before pulling away so fast that the rotten stench of rubber left a smoky outline in the afternoon. Kay reckoned the cops were energized from their Easter camping trips where they hadn't had to look at one disobedient brown face. She said after every holiday, police came back in a frenzy of superiority after days of brandy and Coke and meat picked clean off the braai, black and still burning. A van had also started to circle the school around lunch times, the boere eyeing from a remove the schoolchildren as they moved between classes or as they squeezed through the school gates a hundred at a time in the afternoons.

Kay was going missing yet more, was more secretive and had stopped dragging her friend to all her meetings, which struck Beth as a brutal and abrupt exclusion. An exile. An amputation? Beth had no choice, really, but to begin devising ways of eliciting information by feeling around her friend's silences.

"Are you coming with to the regional meeting at three, or do you have another meeting?" *Kay had already said she would not go with her.*

"Uh . . . ja . . . a meeting." *Not a meeting, but related to politics.*

"I was just thinking the other day, do you still see that guy, whatshisname . . . Karl?" Karl was a few years older than Kay, had refused compulsory military service for white men, so was now a conscientious objector or something. Beth had seen him collecting Kay from a meeting in a rusting Volksie Beetle that barked itself to life and snarled as it drove away. Beth'd disliked him instantly because Kay's new boundaries coincided with his entrance into her life.

"I bump into him sometimes, why d'you ask?" *Yep, Karl was in.*

"I thought I saw him outside the school just now, but I must've been mistaken."

"You saw Karl outside the school?" *Definitely.*

"Not sure, I've only seen him a couple of times . . ."

"Beth, you must be sure man, he's got blue eyes and long blond-ish kinda hair. Kak car. Now was it him or what?" *Whatever their mysterious sessions were, not only were these important to Kay, but they also made her jumpy and that was saying something.*

"Uh, don't think it was him, cos this guy . . . well, I think he had dark brown or black hair . . . ja, he wasn't a whitey . . ."

Kay went back to scribbling lyrics or poems or daily updates, whatever she did in her diary. She was never without the thing; even as they sat together during break, the little book distracted her. But now her pencil started to tap wildly against the cement stairs, until finally she made an excuse, saying she'd be back soon. Beth followed Kay to the school gates, where she watched her interlace her fingers through the wire fence, pushing her nose almost all the way through, so she could look down the road in both directions. Of course, there was no Beetle, no Karl, because Beth had made it all up.

Just as Beth took her seat again on the stairs, the thought hit forcefully. Karl and Kay. Kay and Karl. Their names fit. What if Karl and Kay, Kay and Karl were not doing anything dangerous, but were in love? And what if they were not training or reading or planning, but instead spending their time alone, feeling each other up and being far away from her? She resented him. That was the word. For stealing Kay.

83

"Where'd you go?" Beth said, when Kay got back a moment later.

"Toilet." *Fokking liar.*

~

It was already twelve after six by the time the bus jolted to a halt in Water Falls. A battered sky shot through with gold marked a winter sundown. Beth's stop was in front of Dawood's corner shop, where skollies mingled with schoolboys around the Pac-Man station drinking cool drinks, smoking loosies and avoiding inopportune questions like 'Did you find work today' and 'Did you pass your exams,' in a tacit alliance between unemployed and soon-to-be-unemployed.

Beth tried to walk quickly, wary as she was of men jumping from the darkness. She'd not even rounded the corner when she felt her bag being lifted off her shoulder. Sammy Jacobs, clean-shaven and smelling like a can of Brute, waved her path towards home in an act of chivalry that made her smile.

"I should have thanked you a few weeks ago for what you did," Beth said. "You didn't have to walk me home."

They walked for five minutes, Sammy a towering sentinel, so the neighbourhood boys crossed the street when they saw them coming and even the pavement specials swallowed their yaps, letting them pass unbothered. And then they were standing at her gate.

He took off his cap.

"Do you think I can visit by you?" he said.

"Visit me?"

"Visit you . . ."

"No, I didn't mean to . . . I was just . . . you want to visit me, Sammy Jacobs?"

"Ja . . . yes," he said, blushing deeply this time as he kneaded his cap in his hands.

"My parents don't allow boys to visit . . . and not men either. But maybe you can walk me home sometimes," Beth said.

Before he walked off, he bowed (fokken bowed, Beth thought to herself, thrilled and dismayed) and promised to wait and see if she were on the school bus each afternoon. Beth wasn't quite sure how she felt about Sammy's apparent affection. She did know that if her parents found out, she'd never leave the house or see Kay ever again. Everyone could see he was a skollie with his low jeans, cap mid-way down his face, and his choreographed roll-forward walk. No, people knew a dangerous thug like that belonged to the Skriwe Flats and nowhere near the houses with gardens. Beth reckoned her parents would call the cops—the ultimate betrayal—no one called the cops, not even against skollies.

Then again, it wasn't like she had a line of boys waiting for her. Her politics made her wildly unpopular. The roundness that had started to strain the buttons of her school shirt made her feel even less attractive. But the smart boys didn't dare ask her and Kay out, while the stupid ones were stupid. The popular boys, well, they were a waste of time and anyway only liked light girls, the lighter the better, with genuine straight hair (not straightened) and without a whisper of blackness. Dark skin was only passable if it came with the right combination of sharp nose, flowing hair, and thin lips, and neither she nor Kay qualified. Not that

85

Kay cared. She didn't need anyone's approval. *She* treated *herself* regally, slapping her thighs and bum as she massaged lotions and perfumed creams onto every surface of her body after her bath, slowly and tenderly, like an auntie preparing a Christmas ham. Anyway, the kinds of boys Kay liked—troubled, brilliant boys who imbibed politics with every breath—liked her right back. She was popular without even caring, which made fools of them all.

Beth smiled. Perhaps it was entirely possible to break every single rule that her parents had set.

The New Beth.

11

CHINA

1960s

Of my years as a reporter what can I say?

I have to go slowly through the stack of twenty-three little black books. (Some are not black at all, actually, for I had to make do with whatever I could find.) I keep them locked up safe, from the smallest (half the size of my hand) to the full-paged, the key around my neck.

Long time ago, these diaries had to be placed under floorboards, behind the cupboard, or pages torn and hidden inside socks. For this reason I can't always decipher my own words: sometimes a patchwork, and at other times purposely obscure to hide their meaning in plain sight.

Here are the facts: After I graduated from university I was appointed a junior reporter at a newspaper in Beijing. By then, the Great Leap Forward was at its end.

And? So? Was it a success? Was China the most powerful economy in the world in under a decade, as the plan had been?

Check the history books yourself (this is not that sort of thing).

But really what the little books' scribbles say about its twenty-something author is embarrassing: a young man more interested in writing poetry and watching films than being productive in the world. Low-flickering revolutionary spirit with this one! And the poetry: lousy, flat, lacking in attention to the importance of tone. Those were the years after the Great Leap when a portal opened and a momentary period of openness began. Here, notes with pages and pages about what may well have been his first film, *Spring in a Small Town*, the great movie written by Li Tianji, made in 1950 or so. Surely it must have been an oversight that it ran at the small, dirty cinema (I caught a cockroach the size of a mouse running up my sleeve). The Party said the movie focused too much on love and had no revolutionary purpose, was bourgeois, and so the film was shunned, maybe banned. I can't remember, yet here I have written that I saw it with my own eyes.

More films, even an American Western—*Annie Get your Gun*. There could not have been subtitles then, but I have written: would make for good soldiers, but what bad-tempered girls in America.

his archive

Here, on and on about a book of American poetry by the poet Langston Hughes. He had visited Shanghai before the revolution, and I found a copy of his poems with a Chinese translation alongside the English. He had praised our commitment to freedom, was supportive of our cause and in return many of us read and loved him.

I might say that life proceeded in this way, with this pathetic wimp seeing films and writing terrible poetry. I might then add that I never did begin to doubt that the best interests of the people of China were always put first, or that my mother's disappearance did not have a darker reason. I had in the intervening years come to believe that Mother had perished of starvation soon after leaving Cousin's village.

There came a time when this changed.

*different lenses
& perspectives*

What did I see as a <u>reporter</u>? I have cut out some of the articles, leaving windows in yellowing papers.

Look:

The revolution under threat from the capitalists!

A headline I once wrote.

<u>You see, the period of calm and openness was short-lived, and</u> <u>we were sucked back into the (old) when</u> a hungry madness of paranoia and fear descended. Information implicating someone or other for their capitalist ways found its way to my desk, offering names, places and dates. We reporters, duly instructed, warned of the coming disaster: that the bourgeoisie and intellectuals were planning to overthrow our beloved new China! <u>It was not long</u> <u>before our false missives (yes, of course, I confess) began to be</u> <u>used to convince the country of this coming betrayal.</u> — *use of words/ translation?*

Across China, people began to agitate, and soon even schoolchildren had organized themselves into groups in defence of the revolution and of our beloved Chairman Mao. The Red Guards. Where others wavered, they acted.

Those brave, beautiful young people captured in heroic poses in the smart galleries on Moganshan Lu that tourists buy in pairs, wrap and take home to hang on their walls—that's them. The young army, really no more than children, marched through China in a red haze as they eradicated, under the Chairman's ever more present eye, the *Four Olds of Chinese Society*: old customs, old culture, old habits and old ideas.

And where was the intrepid reporter? Notebook and pen in hand, I marched in step as books from another time were ripped to shreds, pictures pulled from walls (unless of course they were of Chairman Mao) and museums, temples, and shrines ransacked and torn apart.

What did I do? I wrote. Here is a sample of an article (of which there are several thousand):

The indignant Red Guards have declared themselves the defenders of our beloved Chairman Mao and of our beautiful Chinese Communist Revolution, which every day is under threat from new and old foes. One glorious red Chinese morning, driven only by self-sacrifice, a group of heroic girls and boys, some as young as ten, stood proud in their khaki uniforms, red bands tied around their arms, and demanded that rightists offer self-criticism for having turned against the revolution. A heartless former landlord was asked to account for his deeds, for his hoarding of grain during the famine and for his bourgeois ways. He was then offered stern group criticism before his children were warned of the perils of choosing the wrong path.) mistranslation

Terrible writing.

Let me say that for that day there are no holes in my memory. It was the first time I had seen the Red Guards at work, and if I had written what I'd actually seen, it would have been this:

". . . the ex-landlord, beaten down to his knees, hands held before his eyes in submission, was kicked by one child after another until his teeth shot from his mouth like popcorn, while clumps of hair, still attached to skin and blood, came away in the fists of the misled (but still very wicked) children as eyes rolled, snot, blood, piss, shit, breath, breath, breath . . . And then they turned on the man's children and showed them no greater mercy . . ."

The things that I saw cannot be unseen and, let me testify, seep ever deeper into my conscience with every year. The Red Guards dispensed their beatings during struggle sessions to writers, artists and scholars, to previous landlords, and to those who were bold (and stupid) enough to stand in their way or perhaps were simply too old to care what became of their bodies but were determined to give their voices and spirits one last victory.

maybe connect to pushing intellectually & conversations of Both & Zhao?

But how, you ask, was all of this permitted? And why did I not speak or write the truth, as my naïve poet heart surely demanded? In part, one may say that a human brain is more or less like a muscle. Once it has been shaped and exercised to a certain thought, it returns first to that thought before any other. Having grown up with the belief that Chairman Mao was the only true liberator of our nation, and that he had to be praised and worshipped (like the emperors themselves had once been), the girls and boys knew no other way, and their young brains could imagine no better option. *– own liberation*

For the adults, for myself, there are other explanations. The Chairman and his soldiers knew that to keep a people loyal you motivate them with fear. Do not forget that there exists a mathematics of brutality where the amount of blood spilled is inversely proportional to emotional resonance, so that after the first

viewing of an act of inhumanity one begins to grow numb somewhere inside one's head and heart, and after the second, third,
and fourth struggle sessions, there comes a time when empathy is
more a burden than an emotion.

All in all, colour drained from my life. Not only because of what I
saw, but because of what I was not permitted to see: books, theatre,
cinema, art, had vanished again. Only eight operas were permitted that Madame Mao herself had participated in producing.
Even gardens and parks had fallen suspect under the Chairman's
watchful gaze, and grass was to be dug up, leaves trimmed, and
flowers ripped from their stems. Beauty of any kind was not to be
enjoyed, so nature was outlawed, because such pleasure (any
pleasure) was a betrayal of the revolution and Chairman Mao. In
that grey slit of time Chinese architecture, too, seemed to flatten
into function.

My work as a reporter was to enshrine the benefits of the revolution or to write slogans for the front page, which in every issue
carried a picture of the Chairman.

Here is the even greater confession: Despite everything, I
believed that a better society was being shaped, and that all the
sacrifice and blood and loathing would not be in vain.

✗ AGENCY
I have started to cut into the heart of it; perhaps into my own
heart. And now you must make of me what you will.

For tonight I am tired and will resume my typing tomorrow if
this machine will endure. I found it at an old second-hand store, a
Remington portable no. 2 typewriter that some Westerner must

92

have left behind a long time ago. Its condition is terrible, its keys yellowed and nearly useless like broken teeth, but still a gift because I can write this story, my story, secure that the nosy woman who comes to clean does not read Pinyin (I tested her myself). After all, few would think it viable, desirable, even sane to write in non-Chinese script, or, perhaps, to even harbour such traitorous thoughts.

Still now, though. Someone is shuffling downstairs.

12

SHANGHAI

In the weeks after the incident with the magazine seller, Zhao was troubled. I watched him from the window as I readied for work one morning, stomping through the maze, his sweater ripping bits of foliage from the bushes as he crashed past with a restive energy. He lit a cigarette, sucked deeply and almost immediately ground it out, only to light another straight away. So he continued for several minutes, until I had to abandon my voyeurism and rush to catch the train.

During the nights, I could hear him rattling around above me and I slept fitfully as the noises leaked from his place into mine, the scraping of a chair, interminable arc of urine against the porcelain bowl, a tap running, the fridge (I guessed) opening, or the television playing crushingly sweet Mandarin pop tunes, too loud no matter the time of day.

He rarely came to my door then, and when he did it was to mourn the lack of poetry in modern China, to complain about Western impudence (his word) at the supermarket, or to accuse me of something that was happening on the African continent. Why was some leader or other not retired, he'd say pointedly . . . writing poetry instead of being president, playing with his grandchildren, he'd say, expecting a cogent analysis, an explanation, a lament. I offered none. Or he tried to press me on details of my life in South Africa: Why no husband, he'd ask. I left him. Why? He didn't deserve all of this, I'd say, so Zhao would laugh raucously and I'd take pleasure in having found a weakness in his stoicism.

During the restless weeks, I took every opportunity that he presented, and even those he didn't, to ask about the incident.

"What magazine?"

"No, the magazine seller, Zhao."

"You are mistaken . . ." he said.

"OK fine. When you are ready, I will listen and I won't judge you. Trust me, I am in no position to judge anyone about their past actions," I said. Who knew, maybe Zhao had once been a Red Guard himself. And then, didn't I have my own stories better left untold?

It was months since I'd left Andrew. Months in which we'd barely communicated aside from a hastily written email from me about a neighbour complaining about a leaking water pipe, and a municipal bill which had gone unpaid. I'd been the one to settle our debts, to maintain relations with the world. Now I was cut free from that life. And I'd started enjoying the sense of being unburdened of it all. Of Andrew. In this new liberation, I was finding I could look at him, my life, past, parents, with a renewed detachment, perhaps clarity.

Are you free to go with me to the French Concession, I called out one late weekend afternoon to where Zhao sat on a bench. His sullenness had lasted two weeks, and I was tired of treading softly. I couldn't remember befriending someone since high school, and I didn't want it to end.

"This is a colonialist's name, not ours," he said sourly but joined me quietly by way of agreement as I hailed one of the city's metallic ants from their patrols.

Not even five minutes into our journey Zhao took exception to our taxi driver's abilities (or lack thereof) and in a stream of English invective commented on his failure to tell left from right, his proximity to the white centre line, his uncombed hair and all-round grubby appearance (Zhao said he must've just left the village and we were his first fleece), his racing through a traffic light (which I'd experienced so many times in the city, I didn't flinch) and the man's nods and grunts in response to questions. When we finally left the cab our jeans were coffee-stained (Zhao had insisted on bringing his Americano), and after he and the driver had shouted and gesticulated about the dirty backseat, the drive, and the expense (I assumed), the very day seemed tainted. At least, I said, it was good to have the old Zhao back again.

We stepped into a tree-lined road that was almost quiet, aside from a rush of distant traffic or the high-pitched song of a bicycle bell. We walked until Zhao's taciturnity dissolved beneath nodes of sunlight falling through viscose leaves.

Did I know the area had been reserved for the French, he asked? Before the Second World War and the threat of Japanese invasion, "Chinese people forbidden," Zhao said.

He stopped in front of a building, and called me over from where I was loitering a few metres behind him.

"Look," he said, "Art Deco," and pointed out features of an old building almost lost beneath a hasty renovation: zig-zag lines etched into solid brickwork, geometric windows and a rising sun above an iron balustrade.

I followed him until we stopped before what had once been the home of the beloved parents of modern China, Dr. Sun Yat-sen and Soong Ching-ling, or Madame Sun Yat-sen, as she was known too. He insisted we go inside—reminding me that Langston Hughes had spoken about visiting the first lady in the book I'd loaned him.

"This was her house?"

"Correct."

"This would have been where they ate dinner?"

"Well, her house! But who were the letters to?"

"Hmm, people say Richard Rive. Hughes helped get him published. I think they became good friends. Rive dedicated his first book to him."

"From your city, like you . . . ? You know him?"

"What, you think I know all the mixed-race peoples of the world? . . . Although, fine, yes, I just *happen* to know people who knew him. An aunty who studied with him, some people who were taught by him, but I was too young."

"You see! The world quite small, Beth. Every person is separate by only six degree."

"You don't really believe that?"

"I do, of course! Us two: you to aunty to Rive to Langston . . . only four degree," he said, before stopping in front of a framed picture of the Sun Yat-sens.

He told me how the doctor had come to lead the revolution, and didn't seem to mind when foreign and local tourists swivelled their heads in our direction to listen to Zhao's sermon. His patriotic pride perplexed me, because he espoused it as much as he undercut it, and I couldn't tell where he truly stood.

We left the house and walked on, past a gallery filled with commercial reproductions. I convinced Zhao we should go inside, to see the walls covered with paintings of the Chairman in ever more lurid Warhol imitations; full-colour Russian propaganda posters with beatifically lovely women and strong men; modern works of anaemic girls with rounded eyes and hollowed bones. I stopped in front of a series of photograph-like prints. A row of young men and women—the Red Guards, I gathered, from the uniforms and armbands—with heroic young faces staring unapologetically into the present. I wasn't thinking, because before Zhao's body even came to a halt, he spun on his heel and went outside, remaining in the parking lot to smoke one cigarette after the other until I emerged.

Zhao walked us towards a park where we found soup and dumplings.

As we ate on the grass, he said, "To me China means everything . . . no children, no partner. China is my life."

"I know that," I said.

"If spare with stories, with criticism, with history, not because I do not see, do not feel. Just protective. This life . . ." he said, finally.

"Yes," I said. I understood.

In some ways, his silences meant there were few intrusions into my own past. No need for the exchanging of histories or the reciprocity required for personal confession.

How Zhao had grown up, where his family was . . . who he was, this man, my friend, when he was not being the irascible tour guide, I didn't believe I would ever know.

13

HARLEM

1953

Dear Friend,

How is your bit of the equator?

I took your advice, went to the library and took out some books so I might observe this flat mountain that you write about: odd perhaps, but lovely as you say.

Man, I do not know when I will come to Cape Town to climb this mount with you. And I'm sorry to hear of the ever-worsening situation in your country and in your city. Take care, I would advise, and be cautious with whom you speak and how you go about your business.

Otherwise, you sure have been busy! Thank you for the fine collection of stories you posted. I am also including some notes along with the original and the one I had retyped (I have kept a carbon here). I suggest only one change: in the paragraph which I highlighted, the main character, Wilma, comes across too proper, even English in her mannerisms despite the fact that she is meant to be very agitated in the scene (I remember you said some parts of your city were more English than England), still, I wonder if you might throw in some local slang so the artifice might slip and reveal that despite her ambitions, despite how superior Wilma from Walmer Estate feels (note: I thought the alliteration used once adds satire but is too sentimental as a title), she is still a person of color and treated as such, after all. Once you have revised let me see if I can pass it around here (there are many who are moved by your cause, more, motivated, and wish you to know that we will publish what we can or recommend whenever we find an opportunity).

More questions from you still! Be patient, friend . . . in time!

You asked also that I continue with my telling so you might understand my current circumstances and why I am called to answer before the American people. And so, dutifully, I resume my story in Shanghai, July, 1933.

It was the fright of my life to find the offices of the journal of a friend torn apart, an axe lodged in the door and papers scattered across the floor! Even though I knocked on every door asking for an explanation, no one even dared make eye contact with an alarmed (black) foreigner in Shanghai!

By the time I found my way back into the day, I must have looked the wreck, fearing as I did for the lives of the people who manned that office (whom I'd heard about from a friend) and now, my own life too. It was a full two hours later that I found my way back to the hotel (usually a twenty-minute walk). After several telephone calls, I learned that the journal's offices had been ransacked by the local police (as terrifying a force as you can imagine). The journalist I'd been meaning to contact, a slight man with an urbane air, was bodily unharmed, every digit and limb accounted for but shaken to his roots, and I understood then that no one was really safe.

After that, every time I left the hotel, I felt the urge to look over my shoulder. Was someone there? Had there been someone there at all? I felt near crazy. The city was crawling with police of various kinds: American, French, Japanese—you name it, the Chinese too, all fearful in varying degrees that communism might spread but each determined to strike it down wherever it appeared. It seemed wherever I went, eyes—curious, hostile, friendly—followed.

It just so happened that the following day, I received a delightful invitation that would not however alleviate the situation in which I found myself. Right after my arrival in the Asiatic metropolis, I had requested an interview with Madame Sun Yat-sen—a revered presence in China, given her status as the widow of the first president of the Republic of China; and indeed her own role in establishing the new China. I had not imagined that anything would come of my appeal and so I went about my business giving it no further thought.

Can you imagine my surprise when, early that morning, I received a note written in the most delicate hand. Not only had Madame Sun Yat-sen agreed to see me, but she had invited me to dinner that very evening. I chose the only fine suit I had brought along to China, and vanity propelled me to the streets to select a red silk tie, which I knew to be the luckiest color of all for the Chinese.

The same gossiping reporters who had kept me apprised of various bits of information up till then warned me that my hostess was under constant watch. Her own brother-in-law was the head of the nationalist Kuomintang (which, you will recall, had murdered dissident writers just a few years earlier and was opposed to the communists), and yet Madame Sun Yat-sen was sympathetic to the socialist rebels; she and her husband were widely beloved while her brother-in-law had a reputation for brutality. It was also said that she was untouchable and in her presence I would be safe. That evening, in a bullet-proof car I was collected and ushered to Madame Sun Yat-sen's home in the French Concession area, where we dined (feasted is a more likely word) on Chinese delicacies of bird's nest soup and thousand-year-old eggs (the tea-soaked eggs are not old at all). Madame Sun Yat-sen had studied in the USA and we found much in common: friends, art, music and literature. Well, I can tell you friend that I have never forgotten that evening and my hostess's graciousness. After all, no living (or dead) American First Lady had ever invited me to no White House!

After dinner, Madame Sun Yat-sen's bulletproof vehicle drove me back to my lodgings while two cars trailed us all the way (the cars I understood belonged to her brother-in-law's army). When I reached the lobby of the hotel, the hairs on my neck rose as I anticipated a bullet, but as my letter writing must testify, this did not happen.

Now, you and I live on different continents and we have never looked each other square in the eye or shaken hands (yet?), but I think letters can establish as close a friendship as regular visits might and I reckon by now I know you have questions for me. Shall I guess at these? If we were seated in conversation this very minute perhaps you might say: well then, Langston, is it true that you had been entrusted with couriering messages from friends—revolutionary friends—in Moscow to Madame Sun Yat-sen, the mother of modern China? And is this the real reason that you paid the lady a visit and were subsequently followed? Were you, in short, a courier or, more damning, an international spy in the employ of the communists?

In answer: let the private record show (as the public one will soon enough) that I dislike the word "spy" and its connotations and I concede to being neither a messenger nor an agent. Whatever I did was of my own volition and always consciously or subconsciously in the service of my people (who answer as all the downtrodden peoples of the world).

Still, innocent as I was, the next time I stepped out of my hotel, I did so with caution. I was more than a bit afraid for this time there was no question of hidden shadows on my back: two men, one a European (perhaps he was American although judging from his look and style of clothes I would say European) who walked behind me and could not be bothered to hide behind a pillar or slink along the sidewalk, no, he trailed me openly. His equally emboldened Asiatic cadre on the other side of the road did likewise. So exasperated, amused and mystified was I with their open pursuit of me that at one point I stopped and enquired whether I could get them a drink in the sweltering midday heat. The greater surprise is that they accepted!

105

How easy might it have been for them to dispose of me in that unruly city, burying questions beneath headlines:

Poet Langston Hughes missing in Shanghai.

Or worse: *International Spy, Langston Hughes, found dead on the Bund?*

Still, a smarter writer than I would have stayed put in his hotel room, leaving only for the most urgent reasons. But here I failed. Anyway, it was almost time for me to leave the city. Harlem was calling; it had been calling for some time as I had only a few pennies left to my name. But my entanglement with Shanghai was not quite done.

The writer Lu Hsun, thought to be amongst the greatest of modern Chinese writers, had invited me to collaborate on a few essays and of course such collaboration would be no small matter. Hsun was under suspicion of being a communist.

Perhaps if you and I were right this minute seated before each other, you might ask:

R: But you knew you were courting disaster?

L: Was I?

R: Surely you knew there would be consequences?

L: Really?

R: Certainly. Within weeks, there might be consequences and also, for decades to follow.

L: Like? (By now I gather you would have thrown your head back, like in the picture you sent me, and laughed at my obtuseness):

R: Well death, arrest, claims of being a communist?? (Two question marks because your voice has tilted sharply).

L: But I am still here twenty years later.

R: Yes, and there are more ways to try and kill a man's spirit (and his legacy) than death.

L: Such as?

R: No, Langston, you are the one telling the story.

But enough with this tomfoolery! We have letters, and these must suffice.

To continue, on more than a few occasions that week of my Shanghai summer (now numbering days before I left) I found an exit at the rear of the building, and without alerting my fellow guests (who I reckoned watched me) I unlatched the door and crept into a blackened alleyway, and in the dead of night amongst people I had been warned specifically against, I tracked a path to Mr. Lu's apartment. In this manner we worked secretly (or perhaps not so secretly) to understand, to name, the spirit that had brought us, two writers from ostensibly different worlds, together. We found we were not so different; our fights for Chinese rights and black rights seemed to us similar and moreover requiring internationalist actions. After all, what are borders between fellow men and women? We resolved that the struggles for liberation between the Negro (and indeed all black men and women), the Chinese and the Indian were one and that together if only we could cooperate, we might all know freedom one day.

~

With meetings and some writing done, my time in Shanghai had come to an end and the day before I left I was to be honored by a group of writers, including Lu Hsun and one who had taken it upon himself to translate my writings. A dinner in my honor? Well, the two burly guards would have to accompany me this time, I decided, and I dressed once again in a fine jacket and tie and let my surly companions trail me openly to the dinner. Perhaps I had become emboldened by the absence of a bullet lodged in my skull, although, as you will learn, my actions were nonetheless the subject of careful observation.

But now look again, the day is pulling the sun across Harlem. I must retire for Ol' Man Johnson is stirring and he never forgets to complain about my nocturnal typing whenever we bump into each other in the lacquer-stained corridors. But what would you have me do, I always reply, when no amount of work can get done above his constant hum-humming and his Victrola on full blast, singing Ella or Billie. (It's true that I cannot work but how could I ever complain against music that is my very motivation?) He knows I jest.

I will sign off and try to write in a few days' time. But exercise patience, as I am due to appear before the Senate and as such have a pile of paperwork; so much that I've had to employ a secretary. The lawyer I've had to consult has more questions even than you, friend. But of course your letters are no burden and I await each.

Yours Sincerely
Langston

14

SHANGHAI

I'd been in the city six months when autumn ushered in a sense of freedom. Finally weeks of rain, burning days and a haze of mosquitoes departed. The city of eternal clouds momentarily paused, too, replaced by some fine clear days. I felt a new ease settle; at least, it was a comfort I'd not felt for years.

I couldn't know on that crisp October morning that everything would soon shift.

~

The South African consulate sprawled languidly across a floor of a high-rise on the Bund, Shanghai's famed boardwalk. The view featured sixty-floored buildings going up in mere months, a thin slice of the Huangpu River, and, often enough, drunk expats leaving Sunday brunch. If I happened to be working on a Sunday morning, which I sometimes was, I'd watch a swarm of foreigners arrive at the city hotel, dressed to kill and trailed by a sea of beige designer-clad children, conceived somewhere between their ancestral countries of Ghana and Germany, China and Australia, Pakistan and Brazil. They were trailed, in turn, by 24-hour Chinese and Filipina nannies. Any diapers were fastidiously covered in frills (no bare baby bums on display through slit pants like I saw on some Chinese babies). The crowd would leave later that day after a feast of rich, expensive foods and too many mimosas.

Our new consul was coolly indifferent. He had a slight stoop and a well-tailored grey suit—that I thought was more appropriate for a high-powered corporate position than for our modest consulate (nothing like the brick-and-steel fortresses the Americans or the Chinese had in South Africa). Despite his pricey threads, I guessed that Arabile Mzila, the new guy, wouldn't identify with or find himself among the expats anytime soon. His sartorial choices, his curt manner distinguished and distanced him too from the mostly South African staff who shopped at sales or the city's fake markets. This and the fact that he made no effort in his first week intrigued me. And by late Wednesday many of my colleagues had become openly sulky, gossipy, calling Arabile Mzila the virgin diplomat (VD) behind his back. It was an initiation of sorts to have a tag bestowed on him. Because Arabile had no known political ties to the ruling party or ever been an activist (the category I was lumped into), my colleagues felt he deserved a belittling one. He wasn't even a diplomatic hangover from our past like many who stocked our consuls and embassies. Our country's peaceful political reconciliation had resulted in this unholy matrimony between the staff and supporters of the old regime, and those of the incumbent government.

Days went by and Arabile volunteered nothing about himself. Like moss in shade, stories grew about how and why he had been bumped to the front of the queue (apparently ahead of an experienced diplomat, our old consul having left for a senior posting elsewhere) and about him having a secret about Someone Very High Up. The Chinese ban on Facebook and Twitter could easily be evaded by logging on to a virtual private network located outside of the country, but consular staff were forbidden from doing this, so the curious took to whatever means they could of learning more about him, except for asking him directly. Someone said he spoke and read Mandarin fluently; none of us could, and so his presence sat uneasily.

When the High Commissioner called from Beijing that Thursday to ask that I take him to dinner on Friday evening, I accepted, happy for the chance to speak away from the office.

~

I asked Zhao to come with me. His moods had begun to improve again, and I was learning to read his silences; to step around them. But really, I didn't want to be alone with Arabile, who had so soon developed a reputation for aloofness. Even taciturn Zhao would be better than an awkward dinner alone with this stranger.

Zhao and I sat at a table in an enclosed private balcony, scanning the Huangpu. The restaurant was popular with expats and Chinese alike, and had an endless menu that pleased the Western palate. In traditional deference to a visitor we ordered an array of delicacies.

The stirring of wait staff and the craning necks alerted us to Arabile and his wife sailing towards us, both either unaware of the stares (his wife was Chinese) or else cautiously unconcerned.

But then, it seemed to me, no matter what room they entered on whatever continent, they'd get a reaction: Shan was striking, with short boyish hair, and moved with an energetic grace. Arabile loomed over her, yet they walked angled into each other, laughing all the way across the room.

Shan was Shanghainese, had studied in the USA where she'd met Arabile, and because she loathed uncomfortable silences, insisted on keeping an easy conversation flowing.

"Your family very happy to have you back home," Zhao said, warming to Shan's small talk in a way that surprised and relieved me.

"You know Chinese girls and their mothers!" she said. "But I have not lived in Shanghai since I was eighteen. And when I came back I had a Zulu husband with me. But really, when you are away from home for more than a decade it becomes easier," she said.

". . . Just think . . . today: a person is free to study anywhere, be anywhere, marry anyone," Zhao said. "Still not visited outside China," he said, sipping a beer.

"It was a different country then, and everything that your generation did for mine, so many sacrifices, has paid off."

"Not enough," he said, so that I marvelled at this loquacious Zhao and their conversation—choreographed though not insincere—in its play of humility and deference, masking so much from us, maybe from each other.

"Have you always lived in Shanghai?" Shan asked.

"Also Beijing."

"Why here and not there now?"

"Memories . . ." Zhao said, so Shan asked nothing more. Momentary discomfiture flitted between them as they appeared to consent to avoid the past.

"You studied in the USA too, Arabile?" I said.

"Yes, politics and economics. After my doctorate, I taught for a little while. But did the studious investigation being undertaken at the office not find its way to you?" he said, beneath a smile.

"Oh . . . you noticed . . ." I buried my forehead in my hand. How transparent we must have been.

"It was hard to ignore the fact that people stopped speaking the minute I came near them."

"I'm sorry. We're a little territorial."

"But my manners, forgive me . . . if we were Chinese I would be in big trouble for my lack of tact . . ." he said, and shot Shan a look.

"You are in trouble," she said.

"It is true, though, I am more suited to business than diplomatic endeavours."

"Actually, you seem to be unusually qualified. Why did you take this position?" I said.

"To be with my wife in her hometown." He wrapped his arm around Shan and nuzzled her, so I looked away, slightly embarrassed and feeling a longing that I couldn't place. For Andrew? For someone new?

The food started to arrive then. I turned my attention towards the banana leaf cones piled with Szechuan-flavoured tofu, fried fish with bowls of spicy sauce, a roasted chicken, bamboo wickers of dumplings, potato mash with chilies in it, and towers of aromatic vegetables.

"Now this is interesting . . ." Arabile said, as the waitresses fussed around the table, crowding around Arabile himself. Shan said something curt, almost too pointedly, so the staff walked off twittering.

"What just happened?" I wanted to know.

"She said he is NBA star," Zhao said, starting to giggle.

"Basketball players are very hot in China," added Shan. "But, I also said he is here on a holiday and wishes to enjoy a quiet meal."

"Seems to have done the trick," I said.

"Well . . ." she drew up her shoulders ". . . Arabile attracts quite a bit of attention."

"Good or bad?" I had become more preoccupied with race here, how all foreigners might be curiosities in certain parts of the city and how black people particularly were perceived, so I'd been surprised and frankly thrilled to see Arabile walk in with Shan.

"Both," Arabile said, picking up a fried wonton with silver chopsticks.

"You get lots of attention as a couple?"

"Of course. In China, I'm sure you know," said Shan, "fair skin is still a thing. So some people are confused or mystified, even sad when they see us together."

"Tell her about the toothpaste," said Arabile with a full mouth, so Shan shot him a look.

"When I was a child there was this toothpaste with a picture of a black man with very white teeth, red lips—a caricature, and frightening. It's long gone but the stereotype persists and I think feeds on other ideas about black people. There are the water-melon jokes . . ."

"Fried chicken ones," said Arabile.

". . . and modern stereotypes and ancient local prejudice comingle."

"Then just to mix it up, there are the NBA stars, musicians, black sports heroes that're idolized," Arabile added.

"And China seems to be at some sort of a crossroads," Shan said.

"No. You have not reached a crossroads yet," Arabile replied, turning to Shan, so the two conferred momentarily in silence.

By the time the food had been cleared away and the evening was over, we'd made plans to meet again. I liked Arabile far more than I'd expected, and their openness—especially Shan's—meant I could speak more freely than I'd done since my arrival about what I saw around me.

The autumn evening and the sight of families and couples buttoned in coats exploring the city in the dark washed warmly over me. I felt light; I wanted not only to be in the world, but in this immediate one with these people that I'd just met. I felt more unburdened than I had in a long time. Happier, too.

The six months in which the city had been home had some-times been challenging because of my inability to communicate ordinary things: what I wanted, liked, or disliked, while ordinary conversations with someone on the street were entirely out of reach (Mandarin lessons had long stalled). Sometimes the distance between my own culture and this one felt as if it could

115

be measured in a million footsteps. Why, I wondered, did the woman who sold fruit greet me as if I were a long-lost friend yet try to cheat me out of the odd yuan, and when I caught on to her, would laugh as if I had displayed some cunning, and, it seemed, saw no harm in the game. There were the unruly queues, no queues at all, so I stood drowning, shouting and drowning, in stores as I tried to pay. And how was I to reconcile attitudes here about skin colour with the reality of every door being held open for me, a brown foreigner? Yet how I loved the beautiful mania for children, so different from my own childhood, where we were to be shushed and only seen.

Despite the ever-present pollution, the city was also magnificent, and enough people accommodating and kind, so when I encountered prejudice I felt I could either ignore it or beat it back with brashness, as I'd done elsewhere, and as most black people did everywhere when confronted with micro-aggressions. I could direct a taxi driver to where I needed to be, have brief conversations in Mandarin with Ayi, know which places to spend Saturday morning and which to avoid. And Shanghai permitted me to review my past life in a way that had been impossible before. Now I felt I could look back on it without the heartache, as if it were a still-life and each element could be gazed at, studied closely and seen in a context.

As we made our way home through the ever-busy city that night, I thought about the pyramid of broken relationships I'd accumulated over my lifetime. And I'd just expelled Andrew too. I was trying to move on and he was hardly on my mind. Then again, hadn't I missed him only hours earlier?

Then there was Zhao, whose presence comforted me in ways I'd fully comprehend when it was, sooner than I could know, gone.

"I know something," Zhao said as we rounded the corner towards our building.

"What do you know, Zhao?"

"She is daughter of ex-mayor."

"Who? What mayor?"

"Shan, of course. She is daughter of ex-mayor of Shanghai."

"Really? You're sure?"

"Sure? Of course. Tao Shan is child to Mayor Tao."

"Oh. Wow."

"But this is not so easy . . ."

"What do you mean?"

"Shan is from what we call good family—when I was born, good family was a landlord's family; during the revolution if you poor or peasantry: good family. Now, good family is for a famous, rich Party family. But Chinese with much influence want their children to marry to help this . . . this . . ."

"Status?"

"Status. Correct."

"And Arabile doesn't help that because he is African."

Zhao said instead, "I remember ex-mayor. Remember him well. His wife liked the fears."

"The what?"

"The fears," Zhao said, elaborately brushing his arms.

"Furs?"

"What?"

"The fears . . . go on . . ."

"She is very vain. But Shan and Arabile," he attempted the name carefully, ". . . very nice. We see them again," so I laughed at the idea of Zhao as my eternal plus-one.

"What is funny?"

"Nothing," I said as we passed by an old woman, cooking on the sidewalk even though it was around midnight.

15

CHINA

1989

repeats
(

Look, I cannot tell day for day what happened, <u>that is for the</u> <u>history books</u>, but it was bad, trust me. Time is an enemy and there is a point to get to, so I must speed this along, jump ahead and come back round.

During the decades that must stick this story together, I went into places that others could not, asking questions that should not have been spoken. I had emerged from the ranks of the peasantry, and maybe because I was a peasant I was permitted to go into towns and had access to information and events that few others had. Perhaps I believed in my own objectivity, which allowed others to believe the same, and like an apparition I watched and recorded silently.

The decades were strife-filled and no one who had been accused of going against the revolution (fabricated or real) was spared, nor were their families.

Only when the Chairman died was there some relief to the bloodletting. I may as well admit that, along with millions, maybe hundreds of millions, I wept in all sincerity. Having had no father . . . well, we all had our reasons. And once the Chairman was gone, Madame Mao and her Gang of Four (now blamed for all the excesses of the revolution) were put on trial.

Still, after his (small H) death, the monochrome of the previous decade began slowly to crack. Some say this was so because of Deng Xiaoping, the Party's new leader, others say that the people had willed it so inch by inch. Either way, cities started to bloom from within once again: the khaki Mao suit and the modest peasant dresses fell to the back of cupboards as girls began to wear their hair a little longer and their dresses a bit shorter and we all revelled once again in the grass beneath our feet and the flowers left to grow wild. Foreigners became visible on our streets, counting among them an American president. I followed President Reagan's entourage, along with many reporters.

After the angry hungry decades, the countryside began to heal and China was on a path of growth. Art, books and cinema were free to be cherished.

~

But I do not know what happened to the years. If I had been a man for whom children were chosen, I might have counted my life in their eyes, but this was not to be and there was no one against whom I could keep a score for my own existence.

I had during those years remained a die-hard newspaperman, and my reputation for being organized and disciplined meant I rose in reputation and respect. Due perhaps also to the fact that I was known to smilingly accept orders from on high while glaringly passing them down until even the neighbourhood cat had his revolutionary instructions.

I had moved into an apartment on my own which had space enough for a double bed, a bathroom with its own supply of warm water, and a decent kitchen (a dream no peasant boy would have dared to have). Now in my forties, I seemed to have extended my youth on account of being single. I had friends with whom I could discuss books and art and culture and who regularly accompanied me to the opera. I ate well, cooking my own meals some nights and on others walking through the food market until I found something. I read Chinese literature and English classics, which were now readily available. Occasionally I met a foreigner as part of my work, but always mindful, we exchanged few words.

But blah blah blah. This stuff is boring. What actually happened? When? How? Yes, I must come to it now.

1989.

I was lying on my bed with a book. I don't remember what, so it couldn't have been of much interest or maybe the events to follow washed my mind of everything that had come before. I heard a commotion coming from the street below. Outside my window, an endless line of students walked solemnly below banners that read *Down with Corruption* or *The People Love the People's Army*. A great wave of irritation passed over me as I grabbed my jacket, notebook and pen and made for the door. It had started months earlier as students mourning the death of a Party reformer, and from there had escalated to daily sit-ins at the square across from the ever-watchful portrait of Chairman Mao (and not far off from his decaying body lying in state). In all these months I had not been down to the square myself. I had enough to keep me busy and anyway there were other reporters to cover the stories.

Why this evening? I do not know the answer, but perhaps because there was word that a hunger strike had started. Or perhaps because the years had finally accumulated in my conscience. But if you expect any sort of declaration, there is none. Not yet, anyway.

I made my way to Tiananmen Square.

I don't know. What did I expect? Foreign agents that I had been warned about my whole life? My very own paper just the day before had written about the handful of outcasts acting under the guidance of the CIA who intended to overthrow the government. Was my mind really so poor that I could no longer distinguish truth from propaganda? Because the sight that greeted me was astounding: Thousands had gathered peacefully all across the square. It was more outdoor festival than political meeting, or wasn't the kind of meeting I was used to, anyway. I saw a young girl seated against a lamppost, her legs pulled up to her chest so a segment of bare thigh was visible; a delicate, expressive face peeked out from a fluffy white jacket. This partly undressed girl brought to mind an anime cartoon more than a foreign-funded dissident. Over here, a group making a big-character poster: *I am completely dismayed that the police are lined up across from us as if we are the enemy.* And over here, someone had taken great pains to write another: *The Students of Beijing University are here because they believe in the right to freedom of speech,* below which someone had scrawled in a rough hand: *Some would say the Students of Beijing University already*

think they have this right and it could be used more sparingly.
Despite myself, I smiled.

Who were these strangers in my land?

Over there, a fire illuminated a circle of young people, singing in English, and when I asked them what the song was, they shouted back: Where have you been? This is Bob Dylan, Comrade. I had not heard of him until then. Here students lay listless after days of having been on a hunger strike. I walked around the square reading the posters that had been stuck on any available space. *Peace, Freedom, Democracy.*

These spoiled brats who had been born too late to have experienced the wrath of the Red Guards, who had never had to eat bark or bitterness, and who had not forgone an education as many millions had when schools were shut during the Cultural Revolution, dared to ask for more?

But, no, I could not hate them for it. Not at all.

City residents had come by the dozens to the square, administering aid to the hunger strikers and offering small sips of water, carried carefully in jugs from home. I walked farther and saw a makeshift kitchen had been established by a restaurant that I often frequented, and was handing out dumplings and soup to students who had not joined the hunger strike. I found workers who had travelled from neighbouring provinces to stand beside the students. Only when I came across a poster that read *Press Freedom Now* did I slump down in the middle of the square.

Was that it? Was that my moment?

Sorry to disappoint, not yet.

I returned to the square each day after that, under the pretext of reporting the events, when really I was drawn towards the coming freedom or massacre (I did not know which) like a bird that understands finally that the gate has always been open, it is for him to nudge through.

Each day the numbers grew and there came a time when the crowd swelled to more than a million bodies. There could be no turning back. Would I, twice in one life, see the impossible happen before my eyes? Would this peasant boy know not only education but now also freedom to speak my own words as I chose?

No, for the army tanks did arrive. Tens, hundreds, perhaps thousands. Martial law was declared, and even so, I did not imagine force would be used against the students with their slightly ridiculous signs and carefully groomed air of revolution. But it came.

You know this story? How could you not? Well, maybe if you lived in China for the past twenty years, then you would not have heard the tale of how thousands of innocents were slaughtered. Because this story will not be found in textbooks, in newspapers, in tearooms, not even on the internet. Historical forgetfulness, meet official amnesia.

what is disseminated

On that day, June 4, 1989, when I could no longer bear my own spinelessness, I stood still and had to bear witness.

I, Huang Zhao, a decent but cowardly man, testify that when the smoke cleared, the beautiful girl who had been seated weeks earlier against the lamppost no longer wore her face. No, it was stuck to the underside of a tank's metallic wheels amid a sea of

124

severed limbs and viscera, or at least I guessed the flattened mess of fat and blood to be legs and arms and guts. I felt a full rumbling laughter like I had never before known spill out of me at the sight of a pair of human eyes rolling in a ditch. Perhaps it was a cry. I testify that the tanks could not have stopped at the first screams, nor when they were jolted with the unmistakable texture of human bones cracking beneath. I testify that hundreds or perhaps thousands—I had lost the ability to count—lay broken or dead.

Either my life began or ended that day. I do not know which, but a sort of doorway opened up to everything else: my life until then, the present in which I found myself, and my mother's disappearance. But when I walked away from the square that day, I also walked squarely into my own life.

16

CAPE TOWN

1989

Sammy Jacobs waited at that bus stop. Every day.

No matter how thoroughly paint had been scrubbed from the zinc shelter, still graffiti and slogans re-appeared. *A freedom to one is a freedom to all* had been painted in elaborate detail—despite the fear of arrest or detention without trial that must have accompanied the art—beneath a solitary fist, muscles and veins carefully etched.

With a chocolate bar in one hand, the other outstretched to carry her bag, Sammy Jacobs stood framed by the shelter: poetic, if not a little pathetic.

Even if she wanted to try and duck him, which she wasn't sure she did, Sammy just came back twice as strong the next day, with two chocolate bars, perfumed and more attentive than before.

Kay had been angry when she'd learned from someone that they'd been spotted together.

"That lumpen!" she'd said.

"What?"

"Lumpen proletariat, Beth. I gave you a pamphlet with all the terms in there to be studied. He is lost to the Struggle. Lost to the revolution. Permanently."

"You said Sammy Jacobs might be a doctor one day."

"I said could have been and maybe could still be a barefoot doctor, Beth. But probably more like an ambulance driver or the guy doing first aid on the soccer field *if* he manages to get clean. But for now he is a degenerate and you can't just somma trust someone like that."

"He fokken bowed when he first asked me out, he carries my bag and always brings chocolates."

"So what, you want chocolates now? Sammy smokes pills, man. I've seen him. He probably sells, too. I heard the cops picked him and a bunch of other skollies up last week."

"So when you said all that stuff about the working class, about communism, you were being theoretical? Anyway, you know he's got problems."

"He's a button kop. A skollie."

"So, you didn't mean what you *actually* said. And, just by the way it's not like you're around since you got a boyfriend. Sammy is."

"Karl's not my boyfriend. He's my comrade. My close comrade . . . I mean, OK, I do like him a bit, but we busy with serious things. Shit. Maybe it was a mistake to recruit you."

"So . . . I'm a soldier now and not your friend?" Beth tried not to let it show how much Kay's absences hurt her.

"Fok. No. Don't be like that. You know you're the only person who actually gets me. The whole picture. You and Karl," she said tugging Beth by the sleeve.

"Ja but sometimes you're more commander than friend. *You* decide when things happen, how they happen. When you can and can't tell a secret. When you get to pencil me in."

"You're my best friend, Beth. But this kak can get you killed. I can't tell you everything! If you make a stupid decision and get hurt, that's on me. We not playing games here. Plus, you know we believe in all of this. We need to stand with and for the people, Beth. It's the right thing to do . . . the only thing for me that makes sense in this shit hole we call Water Falls. Ever wonder where the waterfall is? The only way I can imagine any kind of future, Beth, is to believe in this one thing. But people like Sammy Jacobs are almost hopeless, and deeply susceptible to being co-opted."

"What?"

"Working for the boere! Working with the police against the people! Pimping on us! It's been known to happen. Often."

Beth didn't say anything to Kay about the conversations she and Sammy had started having. How much she looked forward to the sight of him waiting at the bus stop after school. That during those late afternoon strolls, because that is what they had become, she'd thought it her duty, her revolutionary duty to educate Sammy Jacobs. She tried to start with the basics, which she herself had only just begun to understand: equality, feminism, the National Democratic Revolution, working her way up to Marx. Although she might not get that far. And he listened, paying attention to her. All her. For once.

Beth didn't tell Kay that he'd asked about her too, often enough for Beth to wonder who it was he was actually after. But

Sammy said he was just looking out for Kay and was hardly impressed that a white guy had started to pick her up regularly in his kak blue car. Other than that, Beth was sure she hadn't told Sammy anything very important.

~

The Volksie Beetle smelled like an inner chamber of hell. There was no air between the tank and the seat upfront where Beth, Kay, and Karl bunched together in the absence of a back seat.

Bit by bit Karl was becoming a fixture of their lives.

They were on their way to a mass rally at a university on the other side of the city. At every bump, every pothole along the circuitous route the trio rose or fell in unison. It was the way Beth had always imagined a horse and cart ride.

Beth was flushed with embarrassment. Her butt cheek slanted up the yellow cushion that covered the metal hand brake, which Karl was forced to activate every time they stopped so they wouldn't roll back. Kay had taken the window seat, complaining of a headache, so Beth was close enough to smell the fabric softener rising off Karl's thick hand-knitted jersey (probably his poor Ma still made and washed his clothes) and to witness his long thin toes tapping in Jesus sandals to the Bob Marley tune playing on a cassette. It dawned on her that she had never been this close to any white man. Only her mother's boss who'd tried to lure her to sit on his lap for a fifty-cent piece, so her mother never left her alone in the old perv's company. Despite herself, Beth had to admit Karl was like no one she'd ever met. He spoke in a soft voice and considered, it seemed,

130

everything beneath the sky with equal weight. The pavement special stepping into the road that he'd swerved to avoid, the old African man trying to cross, repeatedly ignored and for whom Karl had stopped a line of cars despite the throng of hooters. He even praised the rain.

And Kay, she listened to him like she was a devotee.

"I think you should read the speech as we discussed it, Kays." *Kays, well that's cozy.*

Said Kay: "But don't you think it will come across as too didactic?" *Didactic? Fokken hell.*

"I don't think so . . . it's strategic but aims to win hearts and minds . . . you did well," Karl said, smiling over at Kay, as Beth pretended to look straight ahead of her.

"You're right, OK." *OK? You're right? What the fok?*

Beth was mad. She hated to admit that there was an unearthing of Kay in Karl's company, a fresh layer of person being revealed that Beth had not seen brought out by anyone else. Not the grandmother who spoke in quick fiery sentences, not the teachers who watched what they said around Kay. Certainly, not with her.

Beth had never before heard Kay speak to an audience. Hundreds of university students and a handful of lecturers piled into an oversized room where Kay was the fifth person on the podium. She would speak about the way forward for the student movement after a spate of arrests.

From afar Beth evaluated her friend, this slip of a girl with steel in her eyes as she made her way to the front of the room.

Kay's fist rose. The room fell silent. No one looked away as she spoke. No one laughed at her earnestness. No one seemed to think of her as a teenage girl at all, nor was anyone especially interested in the bangles that ran to her elbow or the T-shirt that outlined her small braless breasts, or the patchwork pants that looked as if they'd been hand-sewn by Karl (or maybe his Ma).

"Listen," Karl said nudging Beth, as he shifted to the edge of his seat, despite that she hadn't said a word.

"Did I then speak?" said Beth, as rudely as she could.

But he only had ears for Kay.

"We are done with requests," Kay's voice was unusually soft, more drone than roar this time, so one had to strain to hear every word, and yet something in her tone scared Beth.

"No longer will we say: we want equality. Instead we will say: there will be no more *inequality*. No more laws that break and never build. No more prison cells. From here on, there will be no pleading or asking. Hear me when I say: no more. No more. No more . . ." she repeated, until the room hummed with the words like a chant.

Beth's mind would drift back to that afternoon over and over again in the interceding years. Kay. The wonder of that girl. Beth had never admired anyone before. How much she wanted to be like her. *Be her.* And then, didn't she hate her a little, too? The way everyone waited on her words. How teachers, boys, even police were seemingly intimidated by her.

Still, the idea that Kay was even possible in that shit hole had to mean something. A poppy rising through dirt. Maybe what it also meant was that if Kay could do it, so could Beth. Claim some human space for herself, become a full person—no longer in anyone's shadow.

~

On that ruinous morning that Beth learned what happened, there were signs that should have alerted her to the coming calamity. The thin shuddering of a voice over the phone. Beth had tried to call Kay early and got her grandmother instead. She'd been furious then because Kay had been a no-show at school. After an initial hesitant hello, she'd heard a series of muffled sounds. Sobs? Before the line went dead and the telephone was left to ring unanswered.

The unnatural hush as Beth walked down the corridor towards Salie's office where she'd been summoned. The sighing of her left shoe as it loosened after a moment of adherence to the red polished surface. The intolerable weight of knowing that something had to be very wrong. Because where was Kay? It was an important day, voting would take place tomorrow and Salie had given them permission to address the students about non-collaboration. Kay had made the notes but had said she thought it was time for Beth to speak in public. As unreliable as she could be, surely . . . surely Kay wouldn't have let Beth down on this of all days?

Beth stood before Mr Salie.

"Sit my girl. There is something I have to tell you. I've been trying all morning to ring up your parents . . . but couldn't get hold of either . . . this news, nothing will ever prepare you . . . I wanted to tell you before you heard this elsewhere. There's been a terrible accident," Mr. Salie said, wiping his forehead with a handkerchief so Beth's mind hooked onto the trail of thin red cotton escaping its warp.

"Sit child."

Why was Salie being so nice?

"No, not an accident. There's been an explosion." He hesitated, so Beth noticed the too-short nails bitten clean down to the skin. "There will never be the right words to say this: Kalliope was killed this morning."

"Kalliope? Who the fok is Kalliope?" Beth said.

"What?"

"Who is Kalliope?"

"*Kay*, Beth. Your friend, Kay, was killed in a bomb blast at Water Falls police station," he said, and his voice broke.

Beth did not wait for him to say he was sorry again and again, but let his words trail behind her as she turned and walked out of his office, her left shoe resuming its incoherent sighing.

She had used the F word with Salie. Holy motherfucker. Did he say Kay was dead? No, he had said Kalliope. Salie had not expelled her on the spot. *Who the fok is Kalliope?* Why had she said that? Kay was dead but she was not expelled. Kay. An explosion? Kay is dead. Not expelled. Not yet expelled. How the fok could Kay be dead and she was not expelled? Kay. Kay. Don't scream. Don't. One foot, two, one, two . . .

17

SHANGHAI

A gothic fog crawled from the ocean, rolling down the city streets and sidewalks so walking felt like a trawl through milk. Winter had descended. Knee-high bushes, cars and statues were rimed in fragile layers of frost.

It was around then that he vanished. No, not around then, I know the exact details: date, month, weather, day. The fifth day of December on a winter's morning, Huang Zhao was either subsumed by an ominous Shanghai vapour, or maybe he dissolved in a puff of his own smoke? The substance of his actual vanishing would remain elusive.

I'd barely seen Zhao that week. An emergency had arisen when a South African couple had tried to smuggle cocaine into the country in a papier-mâché giraffe. All my time and energy were required to study the infinite complexities of Chinese law. With the threat of a death sentence hanging over the couple, I'd had to be on constant duty, attend to minute details, notify families and have legal representation on hand. I didn't sleep much, and when I did, I awoke intermittently to dreams of buses, trains and planes departing a moment too soon, leaving me stranded and alone in grey waiting rooms.

That Friday, an emotional and physical torpor spread over me and I climbed into bed at seven p.m., not stirring until my doorbell rang at six the following day. Even for Zhao I reckoned that was early. But no, it wasn't him.

At first I thought another stranger had come to my door. It took a moment to place him. While names are elusive for me, faces always leave an outline.

I had seen the man months earlier, speaking to Zhao the day I'd followed him into a hotel and where they'd had a heated conversation. I'd never thought to ask Zhao about the incident, had all but forgotten it, yet here stood his friend or his enemy (frenemy?) at six on a Saturday morning.

He spoke no English, or so he implied with exaggerated gestures as he pushed an enormous old typewriter into my arms, an envelope pursed beneath its metal lip. Then he was gone.

Despite its bruises and yellowed teeth, the typewriter was a thing of great grand beauty. Old and heavy, an antique. I placed it in the centre of the glass-and-steel dining table that had come with the apartment. Inside the envelope were the book of letters I'd loaned Zhao and a slip of paper addressed to Elizabeth, the full name I couldn't recall telling him.

✱

Thank you.
For friendship.
And melancholy too.

136

He'd left a dog ear on a page of the book. I opened it:

Dear Friend,

The ocean stretches far before me now with not a ripple out of place. Man, it's a wide blue sea with houses that hug silver sands winding along miles of coastline.

He hadn't finished reading it?

Neither stopping for a jacket nor shoes I took the stairs two at a time. The front door of Zhao's apartment was ajar so I nudged it fully open. I'd never been to his apartment before; hadn't been invited, in one of the unwritten laws of our friendship that we were to socialize in my domain only. A team of people were inside his place holding mops, dusting cloths, brooms, and other cleaning implements that took me a moment to place. There was no furniture. There were no cups or papers or pots, no detritus of any sort. There was no Zhao. He was gone. Had always been ready to go and I realized then that I'd always known this about him.

I tried to ask if the people cleaning knew where he was, but everyone shrugged or grumbled beneath their breaths: not our problem, crazy foreign lady without shoes and a jacket in this cold.

My feet were turning blue, I noticed, as I walked back to my apartment, chipped Berry Red polish cracking open the concrete sea. I felt a sudden chill from the cold that blew into the city, gathering in the corridors and unfilled corners of the block. Maybe emanating from the passages of time itself. I thought I'd make it to my apartment, but before I reached the front door, a terrible ache that started in the region of my solar plexus (my actual soul?) grew intense, spreading through my entire body, so I slumped against the wall. There I stayed, feeling my loss, my losses, the way I should have done for Andrew, as I couldn't remember having done since Kay's murder. For all of them and myself too. How long did I sit there turning blue? I might have frozen to death had the handyman not walked by and started fiddling with a loose drain or something directly in front of me, all the while pretending I wasn't losing my mind half a metre away, so finally I clambered up and into my place to escape him.

Had I forgotten? I should have remembered that friendships, people, were not to be trusted. Hadn't I learned this lesson already?

connection

PART 2

The past and present wilt—I have fill'd them, emptied them.
And proceed to fill my next fold of the future.
Listener up there! what have you to confide to me?
Look in my face while I snuff the sidle of evening,
(Talk honestly, no one else hears you, and I stay only a minute
   longer.)
Do I contradict myself?
Very well then I contradict myself,
(I am large, I contain multitudes.)
I concentrate toward them that are nigh, I wait on the door-slab.
Who has done his day's work? who will soonest be through with his
   supper?
Who wishes to walk with me?
Will you speak before I am gone? will you prove already too late?
                    "Song of Myself," Part 51, Walt Whitman

A thousand villages overgrown with weeds, men wasted away;
Ten thousand homes where only ghosts sing.

                                        Mao Zedong

18

SHANGHAI BOOK CLUB

I received the first of the files in an unmarked manila envelope on a Monday morning, more than a month after he'd left. About to leave for work, I saw it folded in half and dangling from the letter slot. No one besides Zhao had ever used that slot, even though Ayi maintained its high bronze shine, attending to it weekly with a small yellow cloth and a pungent concoction. My personal mail was posted to work, and the copper slot was ornamental, or the conduit for Zhao's voice to swim through the flat when he came to visit. A few seconds after knocking, he'd flap the letterbox repeatedly, before pressing his face against it to shout: *"Ni hau! Ni man lai.* Very very hungry this morning and no coffee!"

But I tried not to think about Zhao anymore. I dug into work, or read voraciously on arriving home—whatever I could find on my shelves, getting to books I'd had for a decade, and now threw open, hungry for distraction. There were the city's English bookstores to trawl on Saturday and Sunday mornings alone now, the books so cheap—I'd heard copyright laws on English books were practically nonexistent—I bought a dozen at a time.

This first envelope to arrive held more than a hundred pages, bound with a rusting metal clip. Some pages had been typed in Pinyin, others handwritten in Chinese characters. No one needed to tell me it was from Zhao.

I called work to say I'd be late, and then sat with a pile of dictionaries left behind from my stalled lessons, Google set to translate. Of course, apart from the occasional word and date combination (1958, mother, home, etc.), the text was impenetrable.

As usual with Zhao I had a million questions: Had he delivered this to my door during the night? Why hadn't he simply knocked? (It wasn't beyond him to disturb my sleep.) Was this the typing he'd been busy with when I'd first met him almost a year ago? Above all, what did it mean?

I felt sufficiently nervous about the papers—why I couldn't say—and decided not to leave them in the apartment. Instead I packed them into my work bag, planning to carry them with me until I knew what they were.

The next morning there was another consignment, a continuation of the first, this time delivered in a wrinkled plastic bag from the local supermarket. On the third morning, yet more, so the bag I took to work became heavier and I resolved that I needed to do something. Whatever the papers were, I assumed they needed protecting, given the way Zhao had simply disappeared. Despite my racing early to the door on Thursday and Friday, there was no more communication, and I was left strangely unsettled.

At the end of that week, I reached home after stopping briefly at the store for groceries, turned on the television, opened a bottle of wine and sat with the papers again, running my finger through the words. I comprehended the occasional meaning, but the whole remained maddeningly elusive.

It was on page 83 when I saw the date, handwritten in black on white paper, that so stunned me I knocked my wine from the table, shattering the glass and spilling the liquid across the floor.

(June 4, 1989.) — Tiananmen Square

The ticks, thuds and reverberations I'd grown so accustomed to that they'd assimilated into the background became startlingly loud and clear: the perpetual building works, the thrum of the air conditioning, taxis racing on the road below, the rumble of the fridge foregrounded by an American TV anchor offering his opinion through absurdly white teeth. I got up, walked to the kitchen to get a cloth and broom, convincing myself that I'd read the numbers wrong. After all, these were the numbers that when so combined were banned in China and forbidden by law to be searched on any website on the Mainland. At the consulate we'd been specifically cautioned about ever raising this date with anyone outside our circles and certainly never discussing it with a Chinese national for it represented one of modern China's most damning days, when a near revolution had been quashed at Tiananmen Square. As the anniversary of the day approached each year, authorities became tetchy; I'd read before arriving in China that people were arrested for having merely been associated with the dead: mothers, siblings, anyone who'd mourned or commented on the murders decades earlier.

What had Zhao seen?

~

143

I don't fully recall what happened next. My fingers must have hovered over the Enter key, uncertain which words I could or couldn't search. Quickly abandoning this idea, I poured more wine. I suppose I finished half the bottle, walked over to the couch and, papers in hand, fell asleep with the news running. What time could it have been when I heard the door slot shift? Two a.m.? Three a.m.? Awaking with a start, I lifted my head unsteadily to the sounds again, so that a surge of adrenalin or some elemental instinct for safety sobered me instantly. I stood quickly, grabbed the knife I'd used at dinner and tiptoed towards the door, where an envelope was being negotiated through the slot. With a series of sudden moves that would surprise me afterwards, I unbolted the door, yanked it open and found the man who'd delivered the typewriter.

"Why are you doing this? Where is Zhao?" I said.

"No speak English," he replied ridiculously, then stared at the butter knife that I'd grabbed and said, "What, you want to butter me?"

"Where is Zhao?"

"*Wo bu jidao* . . . I don't know . . ." he said, trying to walk away.

I grabbed his arm and spoke louder, "Where is Zhao?" and caught a glint of panic in his eyes. Any louder and someone would be on the steps at any moment.

"Zhao is gone," he said. "He asked me to bring you the papers. I cannot keep them anymore. He said you would want them."

"I do want them, but I don't understand what they are saying . . . I barely speak Mandarin. Are there more? Can you help me translate?"

144

"No, I am finished now. The papers are yours and also your problem. I want nothing more to do with them," he said, and started to walk away as a light at the top of the staircase switched on and a voice called down.

"Wait, please. Is Zhao all right? Is he safe?"

"For now. But you must worry about yourself," he said, before moving swiftly into the darkness of the stairwell.

"Sorry!" I shouted up. *"Du biqi!"* I said, as the door above slammed shut. My head was spinning. Certainly from the wine, but also from the realization that I was a diplomat in a foreign country and had just begun to harbour writing and thinking that was expressly forbidden here.

When I finally crawled into bed, my dreams were again of airports, bus stations, and train stations, arrivals and departures filled with people from every stage of my life rushing about, ignorant of my paralysis.

By the time eight a.m. came round I was out of the apartment. My night visitor couldn't have entered the secure high-rise unseen by the surveillance cameras or 24-hour staff and I knew I'd have to be careful from then on. Instead of taking the elevator I walked down the many flights of stairs and left through the back exit. I slipped past the two women on duty, who were deep in quiet conversation.

Over my shoulder I carried a bag of subversive or dissident writings—I couldn't be sure. I was nervous because it was said that the authorities didn't care what was said about China outside of the country, only what was said within it. The bag began to knot my shoulder as I made my way across town. At my office building, I passed it through the scanner. It was Saturday, so the regular security guard was off and I felt relief at being spared small talk and his practicing of English clichés and sayings that he'd collected like stamps from other expats.

In my office I locked the files in a cabinet, adding an additional combination lock to the outside. I don't know. Did I start to tremble? Did I raise my hands to my face and cover my eyes? What had Zhao sent me and why? The knocking snapped me back to attention.

"You in today?" It was Arabile Mzila.

Arabile sought out only me for chats, and his reputation among the rest of the staff as an interloper persisted.

"Had some paperwork to catch up on . . ." I said, shuffling documents on my desk.

"Good, because there is something I want to speak about." Arabile walked in, seemed to stare at the newly secured cabinet, sat down and pointed an expensive leather brogue in my direction.

"I know it's late notice, but Shan and I would like to invite you to our place. Just this morning we decided to have a few friends over for a dinner party. You should bring your friend, Zhao too. Shan really liked him. I had planned to call . . ."

"Sure, yes, that sounds lovely. Thank you," I said, pushing to the back of my mind the excuse I'd make about Zhao's absence.

~

146

The taxi ride to the French Concession left me feeling out of place. Melancholic. The last time I'd been, Zhao and I had come here together.

I'd not been sleeping much, or when I'd managed a few hours, been awakened by dreams of my youth, Kay, the TRC sessions; all part of a past I'd tried never to visit consciously. Because when something did remind me of her—an odour, song, a glimpse of someone who looked like her—I'd become immobilized, almost stricken with grief. Now the memories returned once again. Nightly.

Shan and Arabile lived on a street of young creatives, drawn to the area because there they could temporarily revel in certain unorthodoxies and freedoms normally frowned upon. Dress and attitudes were less stringently watched, people dabbled in the arts and experimented with life in ways they were unlikely to do elsewhere. As I stepped out of the taxi into the crowded street, trying to locate the buzzer in an overly ornate geometric lattice door, I thought how much Zhao would have liked its Art Deco features, before shoving down the idea.

A small group, mostly foreigners, were standing in their socks and stockings, gathering around the apartment's centre island, chatting about global politics, work, Shanghai's wonders and peculiarities. The room's wide empty spaces, slim couches, and monochrome rugs; the Senegalese music playing softly in the background; the trays of sushi, fried chicken, dim sum, placed the party everywhere and nowhere.

147

Arabile was casual in jeans and a T-shirt, but no less imposing, no less serious than at work. It was only in Shan's company that his edges started to smooth and one saw the outline of where another man began.

"Where is Zhao?" Arabile said, as he took me around introducing his friends.

"He had to leave suddenly. Out of town," I said.

"What a pity. I enjoyed him," he said in the way people did these days, "a definite character. Shan thought your friendship looked . . . interesting."

Shan and Arabile's friends could count themselves among the world's floating educated class, taking opportunities and work as they arose, bartering fluency in several languages and first-class university qualifications, living in countries which a decade earlier would have been unthinkable or inaccessible. Despite my constant worry about Zhao and the papers, it felt good to be with people of my own generation. When Kamal, the Pakistani-English writer in jeans and navy blue jacket, visiting the city on a fellowship, followed me across the room on a few occasions to talk, I felt flattered. I was in my late thirties, and remarriage, children even, hadn't slammed the door on me. Yet midway through the evening Kamal took a phone call, disappeared for half an hour and on returning didn't speak to me again. His sudden disinterest stung, but only just coming as it did beneath the weight of having lost Andrew.

We were watching Arabile prepare a dinner of chili tofu, glass noodles, seared beef and peanuts. A guest, and as I gathered from the talk, a distant acquaintance who'd arrived with a mutual friend, was holding court.

"But honestly, from what I've seen the Chinese couldn't handle democracy," Deidre said. "I mean not you, Shan. Of course, not you! But you know, a disabled colleague was pointed at . . . stared at in the street the other day. Where is the respect for individual rights? And until then . . ." she continued into a wall of stunned silence.

I knew these conversations and attitudes . . . had heard them spoken openly at gatherings of the international community that I was often delegated to attend on behalf of the consul. And this was the main reason that I went out of my way to avoid such events unless compelled by duty. No matter, the talk followed one to the fruit and veg aisles of the local stores. There it was, in the quick glance or knowing nod between foreigners: you see, look at that . . . they're not like us, never have been. Now, before our Chinese host, the words, their intention amplified.

Arabile softly told Deidre to stop, and the embarrassed friend who'd brought her tried to speak over her, but Deidre's silence could not be negotiated as she refilled her wine glass.

"And the spitting! Someone lobbed a ball of spit right at my shoes last week . . . in a mall! The man wasn't even being rude, just doesn't understand that this is uncivilized by Western standards," she said.

On it went until, finally, Shan interrupted.

"Deidre," she said, with an exaggerated Englishness, stretching the name until it felt as if it was about to snap, ". . . of course, there are things even I, a Chinese person, dislike," Shan said. "But after years in many different countries one must . . . if you have any sense of fairness . . . you must excuse that which you do not like or cannot understand, cannot contextualize. For instance," she said, fastidiously wiping the counter, "one sees vicious ignorance from certain foreigners in Shanghai who consider the Chinese beneath them: uncouth or savage. And then, some Chinese regard the expats as the barbarians, unable to appreciate nuance during social interactions . . . prejudice. No more, no less from either side. I excuse you, but I shall not tolerate you," she said, and showed Deidre the door.

I liked Shan more for it.

~

Later we sat on the balcony, as Shan smoked a thin brown cigarette. She asked about Zhao.

"Where's that lovely old fellow . . . I can call him old, right, you're not romantic?"

"Oh good lord, no," I said. "He is grumpy. And finicky. And I seem to think gay."

"Well, why didn't you bring him with?"

"Actually, he vanished, Shan," I said, uncertain why I'd told the truth. Was it to test her reaction? Was it the wine? Or had I already begun to engage her in a situation that would lead us all down a perilous path?

"What do you mean? Disappeared?"

"He was simply gone one morning."

"Gone?"

"His apartment was empty—I had no idea that he was planning to leave. But one morning, someone, a friend of his, comes to my place and hands me a note. Zhao by then was long gone."

"No word on where he would be?"

"No."

"Maybe he didn't know how to say goodbye. Then again, didn't you say he'd once been a journalist . . . ? "

"What do you mean?"

"Come now," she said flicking cigarette ash into a bowl.

"You mean political dissidents?"

"Maybe. But even people with different ideas can get taken in for questioning, or coerced into compliance. It's one of the political undercurrents which keeps us, upper Earth inhabitants, thinking all is well."

"How do you live with that?"

"Stay low."

"Zhao said your father was once the mayor."

"Yes, it's true, I thought he might work it out. But I am no *fuerdai*," Shan said.

The second-generation rich were the offspring of wealthy business tycoons, landowners or Party officials, and had collectively become known as the *fuerdai*. As quickly as they'd entered the Chinese imagination, the group had taken on a widely loathed identity for their outlandish behaviour. If one kept an eye on social networks and gossip columns there'd be a story about the *fuerdai*'s excessive consumption of champagne that cost more than what a waitress made in several years, shopping sprees from Paris to Tokyo, their audacity, or their general entitlement to everything under the Chinese sun (there was no shortage of sun for them).

I already knew from Arabile that Shan had trained as a lawyer and recently founded a small practice lobbying for women's rights.

channels of communication & how it's disseminated too

"Your work's dangerous?"

"Depends," she said.

"On what?"

"On who I piss off."

"And? Have you pissed anyone off?"

"All the time," she said, smiling. "China can be rough."

"Most places . . ."

"But it's home. My parents are old."

"Shan, do you think that Zhao's disappearance could have been linked to something political?"

"Maybe. But, I am sorry, Beth," Shan said, rising, "Arabile needs me to help him in the kitchen." I could see through the French doors that Arabile was on the other side of the room, scrolling through his music collection for a particular song.

Before she re-entered the buzz, she turned and said, "You know these conversations are not advisable."

Hailing a taxi at 3:30 that morning, I felt easy in a way I hadn't since Zhao's disappearance. But then, I figured with a bit of persuasion, I'd found an accomplice.

19

CAPE'S CONFESSION

Grief blotted all the light. Only ever letting in a ray at a time, if that, before guilt shut it out again.

Grief and guilt. Guilt and grief. But if you're resolute at this thing called life, you learn to live under the twins' miasma.

~

Please could you speak directly into the microphone, says the head of the commission. His black gown flows from his neck in fat pleats, the folds ironed hard and straight.

And when you are ready just begin, just tell the story like you remember it, he coos, and for a moment it seems as if he's invited me into his lounge and over a bowl of biltong and bottles of Coke, we will chat. He is too kind for this line of work, I think, as I watch him wipe his forehead neatly with a handkerchief, despite the cold outside and the fact that I'm the first person to testify this morning.

I'd read the notices inviting people to make statements to the Truth and Reconciliation Committee months earlier: hand-illustrated posters at my local corner store had read: "Silence is Complicity," "Speaking is Healing." Offices had been set up around the country, encouraging people to tell their stories about apartheid, the pain they'd suffered, missing relatives or—even—to confess to harm they'd caused. The great post-apartheid reckoning.

Who knew such a simple appeal would lead rows of people from the quietest passages into daylight? Even mass murderers who'd twisted and defaced bodies for fun as they'd drunk beers and roasted meat, had come forward to cleanse their souls, or at least to confess in the hope they'd avoid jail time. Though it had been almost eight years since Kay's death, her memory, presence, clung. So I knew it was time to answer the questions that only I could, and ask the ones I alone had.

I spy the geometry of my commissioner's handkerchief, flattened in a quadruple fold. His soul is quite naked for all here to see: the people seated on rows of plastic folding chairs behind me, those in the gallery on long wooden benches, the stenographer with her fingers poised, and the silent judgment of the television cameras. Surely everyone sees from the front-page photographs, the nightly news coverage how the testimonies trouble him: the tales of missing children and parents, worse, cracked human bodies that crawl home behind him and will not be ignored; how tired he is of trying to absorb the sorrow of perfect strangers though he can do no less.

I flip through the countless newspaper articles about her death, the insinuations, the outright claims and the pages I've been writing and rewriting about Kay's murder, my role in it, for the better part of a decade. So I will not slip up.

Name? Date? Address? he asks, smiling when I say I've recently been employed as a communications officer in the Presidency.

We are about to begin but my throat is dry, so dry that I find I cannot speak. I'm proverbially lost for words.

Just take your time, the commissioner says with practice, with care.

I clear my throat, taking a sip of water from the glass that is filled to just beneath the brim. How long has the water stood gathering the dust that floats on its surface? Has someone else already taken a sip? Trembling, I drink the entire glass without stopping.

I met Kalliope when I was fifteen. She was sixteen already and a year ahead of me at school, I say into the mic. Kay and I became best friends.

Kay, is that what you called her? he asks.

What she called herself. She found Kalliope too pretentious. At one point she tried to insist that we should call her the letter "Y," inspired by Malcolm X or Khoisan X. "Y" the letter, as much as the question . . . but it didn't really stick.

A soft chortle falls from the man while the crowd behind me bursts into unexpected hilarity. Anything to soften this moment, their giddy hysterics say, and I'm surprised at their lack of hostility given all that has been written . . . said, about me.

I wait till they've stopped.

She wasn't like anyone I'd ever met. Like no one I expect to ever meet again. Kay's vision for our world eclipsed our daily reality.

The silence in the room amplifies my practiced tone; a shell of words, is that all I can muster for Kay? I turn my written testimony face down.

Take your time, he says.

I begin again, off script: She was my friend, but well, actually—is it strange to say—also my hero? Only a year older, I say, patting my hair, suddenly self-conscious that it's gained volume in the cold. She came from the Skriwe Flats—at least, that's what we called the rougher side of Water Falls in Afrikaans . . . because it was so run-down.

The peanut gallery is easily amused.

I came from the houses at the other end of the area. They were small, but considered middle-class because we had gardens. Many were well-tended, the houses painted, my parents said they made the best of what they were given.

The rows behind me hum and click their admiration. They are a participatory lot who would be equally at home in a theatre as at my confessional.

The Skriwe Flats was a parallel universe: inverse to the city of mountains and forests in tourist brochures. Nothing green. Just front doors that led to tarred roads and cement walkways. A bit of bare brown veld was all that really tied us to Cape Town.

Who was it that Kalliope lived with in the Skriwe Flats? he asks, his language too urbane for Cape Town's "r's" which must be spoken from the viscera, rocks of salt in the mouth.

Her maternal grandmother. Her mother worked in Johannesburg, while her father had been tried and arrested for attempting to bomb a police station.

He shuffles his papers.

Her father was William September who spent ten years on the Island until 1990?

Yes.

I turn around and find my parents, close to the front, despite their anguish about everything that's happened: my role in all of this and I guess the neutrality, the impartiality—now thwarted— with which they'd chosen to live their lives. Still, they wake each morning early, dress in their Sunday best and are among the first in the hall so they will not miss a word. This is how they accept guilt, or perhaps responsibility? Show their almost invisible— certainly their impartial—love.

Continue . . . and tell me, us, a little more about your friend- ship. We would very much like to hear whatever . . . whatever it is you have to say, and for emphasis he lilts his voice as his hands draw his magnanimous spirit in the morning air. Do not be afraid of small details, he says.

She changed everything for me. Before Kay, I lived . . . subsisted really, in a kind of slipstream.

Nca! A woman behind me gives her approval. Now that I know that my audience wants to be entertained, I will woo them slowly, winning them over for what must come.

My dreams were between the pages of books. I read to escape my daily life because I didn't believe there was any possibility in reality. I knew that I wanted something more; a different future. So I asked around about political organizations, which eventually lead me to Kay. She showed me that we could envision whatever we wanted, but if we did so, we would need to fight. I joined the student movement at her encouragement.

The Western Cape Students Movement?

WECSMO. We believed in acronyms.

On cue they chuckle.

I attended meetings, helped organize mass meetings, protests. I pamphleteered. Basic things that the student movement required of me.

Anything else, he asks with some scepticism, so I understand he's already read my submission.

Occasionally, when it was required, we did more. I built a burning barricade of tires across the main road of Water Falls once. Just before the elections we needed to make our presence felt. We wanted to dissuade people, coloured people specifically, from voting in the sham local elections. We wanted them to have a sense of solidarity with the African communities, who of course would not be given even this deceit of a meaningless vote. Our aim was to undermine the government's divide-and-rule approach.

Was everything you did well thought out and planned?

I believed so at the time.

Was there any outside influence or was it you students who planned everything?

From what I knew, Kay was part of other structures and maybe took orders from higher up. Whenever Kay returned from weekends away or meetings, she had new ideas, instructions, I'd say.

He looks at his watch. The crowd has been seated for almost two hours, having waited for the commissioner, the stenographer, other little disturbances. I sense the foot-shuffling that will soon begin as the crowd wills icy jugs of synthetic orange juice, plates of thin biscuits with smatterings of margarine being carried to the trestle tables outside the hall for teatime.

I know I need to say it. To name it. As does he, because he doesn't look at me now. I say:

I've been accused by someone of betraying Kay. But I didn't give her a faulty bomb that blasted her into a million pieces. Her death then, now, follows me every day.

Does it? he asks, softly.

After she was gone, nothing could be thought of as normal, if there'd ever been such a thing. The sadness never let up: waited beneath my eyelids, watched when I went to school, when I spoke, breathed on my behalf. Some days . . . many in the beginning . . . it became easier to stay home staring at the ceiling. The Peanut Gallery is silent.

With that he adjourns early for tea with a slight wave at the guards, leaving the crowd on a knife's edge. They must not be made unnecessarily tired, my audience, because this is taxing work. To hear story after story of complicity, of lost children, parents, of death, torture. It is taxing.

The scraping of seats accompanies a fresh barrage of chatter, and the woman who is seated so close to me that I can hear her breathing through her teeth repeats ". . . slipstream . . ." as she heads for the drinks and biscuits.

Only my commissioner and I remain seated. He rests his face in his hands, and I know that he is praying for me as much as for my blighted soul.

20

BENEATH YELLOW MOUNTAIN

Forty-five years since I saw my home village. A lifetime for a man who could think of nothing else in those long decades. A thought impossible to dislodge: Mother.

My journey from the city back to my home village started on a slow train, with seats that felt like a fall from grace. The whole night I breathed in strange people and exhaled their sad lives. Not even a bottle of wine could remedy my epic journey. I tried.

Nothing remained of that place in my head. Terrible had been supplanted by hopeless. The emaciated trees were all but gone, replaced by electricity and telephone poles; the old buildings had been demolished, the river had dried up; where once there were fields of wheat there were now factories pumping candy-coloured clouds into the air.

I waited for a taxi, ten, twenty minutes, until a food vendor, taking pity on the town fool, I suppose, suggested it would be quicker if I walked. The rickshaw men are around the corner, she added, laughing, and as if this were not enough: What do you want here? You lost?

After a rickshaw ride, I arrived at the motel, stored my bags, unpacked my few things and placed my books on the small desk, which overlooked the street. I felt a pang of heartbreak for my typewriter, old fool that I am. Also for my friend. If she'd not suddenly appeared one day, somehow bringing hope, would I have had the courage to come up with this scheme?

I found a place to hide the few journals I always carry with me (the others are stored safely). Then I set out at midday to see what had become of my village, as the sun, sieved through smog, beat down. I was out of breath in a minute. The air was so thick with the neon cloud that rose unrelentingly from a chain of factories at the town's end that a bitter taste hung on my tongue and could only be usurped by poisons of my own choosing. I worked through a pack of smokes in an hour. The food stalls were already open and I found an ancient couple selling hot bean noodles that tasted of childhood. Past the rows of chickens, their surprise at losing their heads evident in their upturned legs that shrieked a mute save-me as I walked by, past the peanut sellers, the candied plums sold on skewers and corn-rice snacks that I had not seen since I was a boy. I walked up and down that main road twice and nowhere could I find a cup of brewed coffee.

Despite its tarred roads, electricity and phone lines, the place wore its neglect like a second-hand suit. Perhaps there were schools here now and maybe precocious children ran the streets, but I saw that the Boom had stopped elsewhere. There were no high-rises, only squat windowless cement blocks; the streets were muddied, the cars old and the people resigned to a lesser life.

I walked until I found a group of retirees playing mah-jongg. I was relieved that this had not yet changed, for on any city corner, any day, you will find a group of old people discussing something of great importance, like the latest episode of *I Am a Singer*, or playing mah-jongg. The conversation and game paused as I approached. Of the three women and four men who stood outside the corner of a barber shop, all but one took the measure of me before they all pretended that I was no longer there. After a minute I stepped closer.

What do you want? asked an unfriendly old woman. Come to spy on us from the government?

No, no, not at all. Good afternoon, I replied, stunned by the sudden inquisition, feeling myself to be their subordinate though I guessed there were only a couple of years between us. And this peasant boy had to confess to himself that here in his home village, the decades away showed acutely. My black jeans and grey T-shirt were almost new, and I saw that as different as I perceived Westerners to be, so was I to these villagers.

They stared at me.

I am from this village, I said, hoping this might appeal to them.

Name? asked the fierce old bird.

I gave her my name, and for reasons I cannot explain besides fear, offered a small bow.

Ha! said one of the men, who until that moment had not looked up. He stared hard, rose and made his way over to me. His beak tried to sniff me out, while his eyes scanned each feature on my face slowly. Without warning, he grabbed my hand and started to shake it violently.

I know you! We played together. It is true, we played Catch the Dragon's Tail when we were boys, well, I was much younger than him then, he said apologetically to the waiting crowd, for now he looked a decade my senior in his dirty vest and woollen hat swelling from his head. You are the poet, he said, still pumping my arm so furiously that I feared I would start to leak.

The hostility seemed to dissipate after this, and they made a space for me to enter their circle.

I could only vaguely remember the man himself, yet recalled his older sister with ease. When I enquired as to her whereabouts and health, he clucked and said that was a matter for a second or third conversation. The rest of the gang, I learned that afternoon, had slowly migrated there over the decades from surrounding villages and cities.

I was offered the only chair with a back and had tea poured for me in a cup so stained that it gave me pause, and forced me to swallow—along with the most excellent tea—my pride. When had I started to fear people like a Westerner?

Play mah-jongg, they commanded.

For the first time in decades I sat with the people of my generation. And why not let me say: people from my own province and village. People who I wanted to call my own.

~

What a journey from the time that I had awoken from my slumber in 1989 to this day as I sit in a motel in my home village. It is not dramatic to say that in the intervening decades I underwent a sort of revolution in my soul (well, OK, it is). Anyway, during

164

those two decades I walked back into my own past. I volunteered for assignments out of town because in the small towns, the villages, the places on the arse of China's stratospheric growth, I could walk right into history, almost unimpeded. The Party had kept meticulous archival records, and from them much could be learned. With my little white card and a picture that made me look the honest and studious journalist I had not yet proven to be, I talked my way into the annals. After all, I worked for the nation's news agency, the Party's loquacious mouthpiece, and had it not been me who'd once slavishly written slogans in support of our revolution? This is how, under the guise of my profession, I was permitted to sit for days uninterrupted and study the data.

What was the result of my troubles? Well, you will have to trust me when I say the past was another country than the one I knew.

All across China people had starved to death while the archives showed that the granaries were full as a Party boss's belly. On and on, in village after village, I saw the same thing. In them as in the village of my youth, thousands of people had died or vanished. The information did not add up: gargantuan efforts by the peasants, granaries which were or should have been bursting, people's communes in which people were to have been fed, fair weather, yet no food.

It was the villagers themselves who filled in the blanks with the barest of prompting as I made myself a street corner veteran joining retirees for mah-jongg, tea and gossip. Perhaps one day, finally, the history books and scholars more erudite than me will tell this story with the attention it deserves. But these are mere

165

recollections, a search for a lost mother, and so all I can say is what I garnered.

The Chairman, praise be to him (my tongue drips), had decided that the path out of centuries of hunger would be by excelling in the production of agriculture and steel. Where others had leaped forward after the discovery of gold, diamonds, or oil, we would be thrown into a new world through our nation's greatest natural resource: the people. And so everywhere people across our country were urged to *Go all out and aim high!*

Orders were sent to the provinces about what was to be grown or manufactured or built, along with targets that had been determined by the stroke of a pen in offices far from the land and the people themselves.

Ride the winds and break the waves!

Double the rice yield, triple the wheat, smelt everything to make steel!

These people have never built a dam before? Then they will learn in a week!

We were in the grip of not only gigantism but also gigantic-itis, which would soon infect the entire body politic. What happened next?

To meet impossible targets, people were compelled to lie and cheat and manipulate not only each other but numbers too (if we cannot make two hundred million tons, we will just say that we can, but someone will have to go without).

To meet the fantastical targets, people were to work and work and work on a sliver of sustenance. Bodies breaking beneath the burden will be a sacrifice to the nation!

To meet the unnatural targets, men in charge took food out of the mouths of peasants, sending it up to Beijing. Or perhaps they locked it in granaries where it would be safe.

To meet hyperbolic targets, everything was smelted: pots, hoes, rakes, all human hours given to the production of steel. What was left on the farms? Nothing and no one. Also no tools and no one to grow food. Finally no food.

To meet the punishing targets, personal thought and space would have to be sacrificed, with communes becoming the new basic family unit of the nation. No kitchen implements, not our problem!

To meet the diabolical targets, complete loyalty of body and soul were required. Should this requirement not be met, a kicking to death would be in order.

Ten million? Twenty million? Forty-five million human lives? What was the cost of the madness? Only the archives know, and they are mostly quiet.

But did everyone only bow and scrape in supplication? They did not. And they died.

21

THE AMERICAN HOUSE

Dear Friend,

The ocean stretches far before me now with not a ripple out of place. Man, it's a wide blue sea with houses that hug silver sands winding along miles of coastline. Summer has found me in Carmel, or perhaps it never leaves here.

I have come to escape Harlem's beautiful cacophony, its endless chitter and stream of people hankering for something: a bit of time, a kind word, any word at all. I am at a friend's cottage; I needed me some time.

Before I reply to your stack of worry letters (which I received, read and reveled in but did not have the wherewithal to reply to then), here is the news of the day: along with your wonderful stories, I have heard from the finest cohort of your countrymen: Phyllis Ntantala, Bloke Modisane, Peter Clarke, Es'kia Mphahlele. The anthology is well on its way to publication and I advise this as a means for the new writer to get his word out, as these go to libraries, colleges and many other places a novel or book of poetry may not go.

By now I reckon you are impatient to know what happened since I last wrote some months back. Well, let me tell you. I bring you up to the present day, and ask that you bear in mind that the past trails us all. Now the reason for my telling of my visit to Shanghai will become clear.

~

I was called to Washington to appear before the Senate, on the heels of having been labelled a suspect by the House Un-American Activities Committee. With money borrowed and a suit that I had saved for from a tour of readings, I arrived to those sessions an anxious man. Already many others had taken the Fifth Amendment so they'd not incriminate themselves. I chose differently. I walked towards the stand beneath the penetrating gaze of Senator McCarthy. Now, let me tell you, though I am not a superstitious man, their eyes felt like a curse on me while the whirr of cameras in the background gave me pause. Still, I willed them legs to walk.

Do your papers say anything about what is happening here?

The reason for the sessions of the Senate was this: copies of books including my own had made their way into American information centres around the world. All around suspicion and caution supplanted reason and kindness. Someone somewhere, in some little darkened corner perhaps, decided that the books should be read to make certain that nothing critical of America was on display. Well, certainly some books were found and thus judged to be treacherous, taken from the shelves to be unlovingly pulped by the hundreds. Poems and articles that I had once

⌐ who gets to write / decide the story ?

170

written and which had got themselves published in pamphlets or journals came to the attention of these men.

What else? Was there a dossier with my name on it that had been collected for thirty years by then? Names? Dates? Meetings? Letters passed (or not passed) between people of different countries? Were there allegations against me? Was the humble people's poet of Harlem to be accused of once having been a courier in a spy network that, say, stretched across the world in the 1930s? A cog—on the side of the communists—in the Cold War effort?

~

Say your name and profession for the record.

Langston Hughes. I am a poet and a writer, I answered truthfully.

And you have written many poems, Mr. Hughes? asked the Senator.

I have written many books of poetry, short stories and novels, children's books, plays, operettas, works of nonfiction . . .

Mr. Hughes, your reputation as a poet notwithstanding, it has come to the attention of this hearing that you have written certain things that may be considered disloyal . . . or worse even than this . . . to the United States of America. And so we call upon you, before the people of the United States of America, to ask if you are now, or if you have ever been, a Communist?

Please could you reframe the question? said I.

Well, it is simple: based on an analysis of some of your writings, I have to ask you whether you have ever believed in communism as an option for the United States of America? he asked, as grey flesh around his mouth pulled and puckered.

Said I: Well, I believed that in America we Negro people were not, are often not, treated justly. I desire for all people, my people, to be treated the same as the next man, the white man, and I have written many poems with that intent, yet, I do not believe that makes me one thing or the other.

So you were a communist? he said, and the flare of his nose, the glare of his eye did not go unnoticed by me.

Well sir, could you define communist, I said, and a line of vapour escaped his ear.

Let's try this: Have you ever attended a communist meeting?

Not knowingly, I have not.

(Frustrated now): Did you attend a meeting at which there were ever fellow communists?

Not that I knew of . . . how would I know if they were communists?

(More frustrated now): Have you ever attended a meeting at which communistic matters were discussed?

Well, said I, could you define communism . . .

Here, he said looking down at the pages before him, his finger tap-tapping madly: Mr. Hughes, are you the same Mr. Hughes that wrote (he took pause dramatically): Did you write "Scottsboro Limited"?

I did.

Was that not what one might call a poem depicting the communist line?

I could not say with any certainty that it did.

Come now, did you not believe what you wrote?

No, not really, I said, in an effort to explain that the poet need not necessarily believe every line that he writes. That it was, after all, a matter of interpretation and perspective.

"All: Rise, workers and fight.

Audience: Fight, fight, fight, fight!

(The curtain is a great red flag rising to the strains of the Internationale.)"

Do you recognize that line? he asked, his mouth bending ever more to misery.

It is from "Scottsboro Limited."

And you say you didn't believe these lines, and yet *you* wrote it?

I tried to explain: The writer, the poet's duty, amongst other things, is to take the pulse of a nation sometimes, to interpret what is being said and felt, and this was a distinct perspective.

Your perspective? he said so fiercely, so harshly into the microphone's ear, that it let out a scream in return.

Someone's.

Did you or did you not believe what you wrote?

Well, in a poem one cannot have one's feet held to the fire and be told to say yes or no—it is a matter of interpretation, as it is with all literature. Simply because I write in the voice of a character does not make me that character. Say, if I were to write from the perspective of a woman in the fields, as I have done, I do not become the woman in the fields . . .

Yes, Mr. Hughes, said he, I understand literature (although I did not agree with him on this matter, I did not say it). And what of this poem, Mr. Hughes, which I don't mind saying is

173

blasphemous, profane, sacrilegious, he said, gasping for breath. I understood then that poems like the following were the reason I had been called.

> *Christ Jesus Lord God Jehovah,*
> *Beat it on away from here now.*

These lines: the poetry of an atheist, a communist surely, he said, so a thousand globules of spit stroked the microphone now. Did you believe this? Well, did you?

Not I, no, but I believed that someone might very well have felt that way, someone who had just about eaten all the bitterness they could from being poor, black and disenfranchised in a country that was said to be theirs.

How do you think Joe Shmoe would read such a poem? said another member of the committee.

Well, if he were to read it at all, and I have come to know that sometimes Joe Shmoe is not much drawn to poetry, then he most likely would misunderstand it, I said, and hoped my mark was hit.

Say, Mr. Hughes, said another still, are you the same Mr. Hughes that wrote, "Put one more 'S' in the USA to make it Soviet. The USA when we take control will be the USSA then."

Well, what could I say to that?

Friend, let me play it straight with you. I made to answer the only way I could.

Permit me a little while, so I may explain myself more fully. May I? I asked them.

Time is short, Mr. Hughes. Speak quickly, he said.

I, sir, was born in Joplin, Missouri. I was born a Negro. From my very earliest childhood memories, I have encountered very serious and very hurtful problems. One of my earliest childhood memories was going to the movies in Lawrence, Kansas, where we lived, and there was one motion picture theater, and I went every afternoon. It was a nickelodeon, and I had a nickel to go. One afternoon I put my nickel down and the woman pushed it back and she pointed to a sign. I was about seven years old.

Very well, Mr. Hughes, said the senator, I see where you are going and let me say to you, there is no need. We know this history, he began . . .

The woman pushed my nickel back and pointed to a sign beside the box office, and the sign said something, in effect, "Colored not admitted." It was my first revelation of the division between the American citizens. My playmates who were white and lived next door to me could go to that motion picture and I could not. I could never see a film in Lawrence again, and I lived there until I was twelve years old. When I went to school, in the first grade, my mother moved to Topeka for a time, and my mother worked for a lawyer, and she lived in the downtown area, and she got ready for school, being a working woman naturally she wanted to send me to the nearest school, and she did, and they would not let me go to the school. There were no Negro children there. My mother had to take days off from her work, had to appeal to her employer, had to go to the school board and finally after the school year had been open for some time she got me into the school. I had been there only a few days when the teacher made unpleasant and derogatory remarks about Negroes and specifically seemingly pointed at myself. Some of my schoolmates stoned me on the way home from school. One of my schoolmates (and there were no other Negro children in the school), a little white boy, protected me, and I have never in all my writing career or speech career as far as I know said anything to create a division among humans, or between whites or Negroes, because I have never forgotten this kid standing up for me against these other first graders who were throwing stones at me. I have always felt from that time on—I guess that was the basis of it—that there are white people in America who can be your friend, and will be your friend, and who do not believe in the kind of things that almost every Negro who has lived in our country has experienced.

Are you done, Mr Hughes?, asked he.

My father and my mother were not together. When I got old enough to learn why they were not together, again it was the same thing. My father as a young man, shortly after I was born, I understand, had studied law by correspondence. He applied for permission to take examination for the Bar in the state of Oklahoma where he lived, and they would not permit him. A Negro evidently could not take the examinations. You could not be a lawyer at that time in the state of Oklahoma. You know that has continued in a way right up to recent years, that we had to go all the way to the Supreme Court to get Negroes into the law school a few years ago to study law. Now you may study law and be a lawyer there. Those things affected my childhood very much and very deeply. I missed my father. I learned he had gone away to another country because of prejudice here. When I finally met my father at the age of seventeen, he said "Never go back to the United States. Negroes are fools to live there." I didn't believe that. I loved the country I had grown up in. I was concerned with the problems and I came back here.

Alright, Mr. Hughes, alright, said a member of the committee. You have explained the emotional background. So, may I deduce that you *have* supported other ways of governing, other forms of government, say even the Soviet style?

Friend, there was much more to tell: but I had said what I had come to say, not to the committee, but to my people, who do not forget could tune into the broadcast.

Perhaps, at one time, I might have wished for another kind of government for myself, for my people, for freedom, I said.

Do you still feel this way? The senator asked, so I detected that the fight had started to go from him.

All they had wanted was some sort of confession? A breaking of spirit?

No, said I. I have not believed in it for a very long time.

Without much greater fanfare I was thanked and dismissed. If there were a hint of more, or, say, an incriminating dossier that told of my spy days, then it did not come to the fore.

There.

It is getting late now, or perhaps it is early, I cannot tell anymore. Only that my young secretary will arrive any moment seeking to wrestle my typing out of my hands. With my conscience finally clear, I bid you goodnight.

Your Friend

Langston

22

THE SHANGHAI BOOK CLUB

If I hadn't fallen through a chink in the known world from the moment I received Zhao's letters, I was at least catapulted from my life. A sudden neurosis or a genuine paranoia moved in. Was I being observed? Followed? My actions monitored and my life surveilled? The city started to feel antagonistic, harsher than it ever had.

Almost every other day of the week strangers started up conversations in a language I didn't speak or engaged me in odd, discomfiting ways.

"Have you seen the day's paper?" an avuncular man asked one morning on the train.

"No," I replied. "Why?"

"I haven't seen," he said, "don't ask me," his change of tone from pleasant to scathing so sudden, I got up and walked to the other side of the carriage. On that same journey the next day, a hungry-looking girl in a flimsy lemon coat stopped me as I disembarked, about to enter subterranean Shanghai.

"Hello," she said with full smile and wide, tetchy eyes. "We can be friends, please?"

"What?"

"Friends? Best friends, you and me?" she said, blinking and digging her fingernails into my hand so that startled, hurt, I pushed it away and walked quickly towards the street.

Perhaps if this had been New York or Johannesburg, where some kinds of disabilities, eccentricity, and even weirdness were neither hidden nor pushed to the boundaries but given place, I might have dismissed the strangeness suddenly engulfing me. But I knew that in Shanghai a stigma stuck to certain mental and physical conditions, and even the expression of originality might be met with wariness.

The idea that I was being observed didn't ease at work, where Internet sites that I'd visited only a day before (harmless ones for books or an independent South African newspaper) became blocked the very next. The pattern held for more than a week and there were days when I checked sites just to see if they would get blocked. Often they were, and I came to believe that like millions across the country, my Internet usage was being monitored; worse, I was being specifically surveilled.

On another morning an elderly Chinese man began to walk beside me as I made my way to the office and said something to the effect of Where are you going? It took my full concentration to decipher that much. But no, I do not speak Mandarin, I said, despite his insistence on continuing in that line. Had Zhao sent him with a message, I wondered? If he hadn't, and if my friend were in some sort of trouble, then I wouldn't speak his name. The man turned just as suddenly and disappeared down a side street.

I still hadn't deciphered much more of the manuscript; how could I? But I bought an additional lockbox, a metal one, locked the papers inside it, and returned them to their original holding place, so now they were triple secure.

There were other peculiarities, such as misplaced bits of clothing—items I was certain were packed in one place, only to find them in another. Books were misfiled in places I wouldn't have looked for them. I'd categorized the five boxes of books that I'd brought to Shanghai based on geography, so Smith went on the same length of shelf as Shakespeare. If there were too few writers from one country, there'd be a regional shelf. Final home country or a specified intention placed a writer who had called more than one country home, so Nabokov got shelved with the Americans. Coetzee's earlier books were in the South Africa section, and later ones in Australia, a decision which had almost made me jettison the entire system. Yet how had all of Rushdie's books come to sit in India? And who had moved Coetzee's latest offerings back to South Africa? I could only assume that Ayi had shifted them while dusting, making subconscious but erudite errors.

There was Ayi's sudden coldness, too. Though we'd started off barely able to communicate, the months together had brought warmth and we found we could communicate quite well after all—her in Mandarin and me mostly in English—about the weather, her new grandchild, and matters concerning the flat.

If I'd done something to upset her, I couldn't recall. We'd never had an uncomfortable moment. Yet now she arrived only minutes before I was due to leave for work, barely greeted me, seemed unwilling to smile, embarrassed to chat.

I knew decisions had to be made. I called Shan later that morning and asked if she'd be keen to start a book club. It was a pretext to get her to look at the manuscripts, so one way or another I could figure out what to do. We set the date for our two-member book club's inaugural meeting: Saturday.

~

Shan arrived at six, smelling of smoke and perfume, offering macaroons from an ornate silver box from the French patisserie at Lujiazui station. She slumped on my couch, tucked her feet beneath her, pulled out an English translation of Mo Yan's short stories and passed this to me.

"Give me a book from South Africa."

"We're supposed to read the books at home and discuss them during our time together," I said. "I thought today we could make a list of books we might read, people we could invite," I added, dishonestly.

"Why speak when you can read?" Shan said, silencing further protest, and began to read *Mating Birds* by Lewis Nkosi, so I picked up Mo Yan's *White Dog and the Swing*.

We read in languorous silence, asking the occasional question about a local meaning or language use, until twenty minutes in I broached the real reason I'd invited her.

"Shan, do books that are subversive ever get published in China?"

"No," she said, not looking up.

"No novels, or any books, that disagree with the standard line?"

She put down her book dramatically and eyed me.

182

"Sometimes, yes, but the use of language or approach to difficult subjects would have to be elusive enough to dodge the censors. If the book does it well, then it may get published. China has many grey areas, Beth. Why do you ask?"

"Curious."

"More often, though, books which really push against something get published elsewhere, Hong Kong or Taiwan or Europe, and are banned on the Mainland." But Shan didn't want to speak, and turned her eyes back to her text.

I prepared pasta and salad, and poured us each a glass of wine for dinner. Before she got ready to leave, I suggested that we walk in the gardens across the road. It was almost nine p.m.

"And?" she said, as we made our way from the building, towards the fairy lights strung between the branches of trees.

"What?"

"Do you want to tell me what is bothering you?"

"Yes," I said, directing her away from the road and taxis where she would soon be heading, and towards the French maze.

"It's about Zhao."

"Not Kamal, that writer you met at my home?"

"No. Why do you ask?"

"Tell me about Zhao."

"Days after he vanished, I received a manuscript, or maybe notes from a diary of sorts . . . I don't know, because I can't read Pinyin and don't understand Mandarin. They were delivered—hand delivered—to me in the middle of the night. Turns out, it was a friend of Zhao's who brought them."

"Written in Pinyin?"

"Yes."

"Why write in Pinyin?"

"Maybe to restrict access?"

"Still, it's odd."

"Or maybe he thought it would be easier to translate for a Westerner?"

"You're not a Westerner."

"*I* know that. Then again, maybe he just wanted to use the typewriter. On the day of his disappearance, Zhao's friend delivered this ancient typewriter to me. It's very unusual, certainly in China, and when I first arrived, I heard Zhao using it in the middle of the night. Anyway, Shan, the manuscript appears to be a story, Zhao's story. I had to connect the dots, dates and words, and only occasionally did this make any sort of pattern. But mostly I don't know what it says or why he chose to send it to me."

But the last part of what I said was untrue. Over those many months Zhao and I had forged a bond, and instinctively I understood that he had not only trusted me, but had entrusted his life to me.

"Shan, I saw a particular date: June 4, 1989."

She sucked breath in through her teeth.

"I saw it repeatedly in one chapter."

"You're sure?"

"Yes."

"Why are you telling me this?" Shan said as we turned the corner, avoiding the barbs and arrows that remained of the usually lush maze. It was still cold, but winter had begun to fade and spring was not an altogether distant idea.

"I need someone to translate it."

"Fuck," she said.

"You see my problem."

"Where is it?"

"At my office."

"Oh fuck."

"Yep."

"It's a terrible, stupid idea! But you have me intrigued. I want to see this script. But I think, for now, until I take a look and think about it, let us not mention anything about it to Arabile. It wouldn't be fair to him."

"I agree."

"You know what you're getting yourself into?"

"Not really."

"Meet me on Monday, at my apartment. No, at a restaurant. I'll text you details. Can you bring the manuscript?"

"Yes, unless I get arrested."

"Well, lucky for you, you are a foreign diplomat. I would say Zhao has chosen his collaborator, or perhaps his editor, well."

"Do you think that was what he intended?"

"See you Monday," Shan said and started towards the taxis, stopped and spun on her heel: "Kamal, he asked about you. Asked that I give you this." She handed me a book: *Silence* by Kamal Khan. I found a slip of paper with a number and email address in its folds.

"He asked if you were available. Arabile thought there might be a husband somewhere?"

"Not really. Not anymore. We'll be divorced soon."

"You need to know that he's separated from his wife and child, who are still in London." And then she was gone.

~

And so my evenings with Kamal began.

I called him up soon. I'd liked talking to him, and I was curious after having read his elegiac novel of betrayal and loss. Perhaps we had a language in common. Anyway, there was the oppressive silence to escape, which he seemed to know.

Kamal arrived always a little before midnight, after he'd finished his writing for the day, and stayed until early the next morning. We spoke about politics and books, conversations I'd missed since leaving Andrew. They were all that had finally remained between us. Was there an idea that this tryst could finally, fully, take me away from the man I'd loved? To have my revenge?

Kamal and I spoke gingerly about the past. When we did it was about the people we'd both suddenly, shockingly lost: his father to cancer when Kamal was twelve; my best friend to an explosion.

I hadn't spoken Kay's name in almost twenty years. I'd forbidden Andrew from mentioning her and tried to live my adult life by relegating her death, all that had happened to her and us, to another time. With Kamal—intimate without being close, compassionate without being empathetic—I found I could speak about Kay without the context of home, and now into the void left by Zhao.

The sex with Kamal was strangely subdued but pleasurable and sensual in its way. Still, I knew we were just passing the time.

He spoke often about his wife and child, how much he missed them but also how he didn't know whether he wanted or could reintegrate into their lives.

"Why did you leave?"

"She asked me to."

"Why?" I asked, as the light from the riverboats on the Huangpu transfigured the walls.

"It's not what we'd had in mind. Marriage, children, you know? She said I just wasn't there, even when I was."

"And?"

"True. I was always trying to escape to the library, the store, to write . . . she needed something, someone, else. So when this fellowship came up, it seemed like a break we both needed."

"I don't think that was reason enough to leave, Kamal."

"I know that. You?"

"I don't know. We stopped understanding each other. Or, maybe, we stopped seeing the same values as important," I said coolly, roiling within.

When Kamal left early in the mornings, he left in his wake an aura of defeat together with the smell of expensive cologne.

~

On the agreed day I met Shan in a Western-style restaurant a few blocks from the consulate that sold freshly pressed juices, organic and whole foods. We shared a plate of hummus with carrot sticks.

I carried the papers in my oversized handbag.

Her face morphed from interest to surprise, to shock, to something akin to sadness all in the space of the hour in which she'd instructed me not to speak to her, so I sat reading magazines I'd found on the shelves of the restaurant.

"And?"

"Damning. Did you know how senior a journalist Zhao had been?" I dipped my head and shrugged. I hadn't really known. "I don't know quite yet, but it looks like a confession of sorts. Here: The great famine." Shan's voice scraped the floor.

"What about it?"

"For starters, he writes about it; Chinese do not speak about these things. We do not write about what we have agreed by consensus, as well as under duress, to forget. Yes, the information comes out in dribs and drabs . . . many millions died, we know this . . . but this personal testimony against the revolution, the post-revolution period, by one who is inside of China, who seemed to have been a mouthpiece. It is significant. I will have to read more but . . . where, when can we do this?"

"I have to keep the papers at the consulate, right?"

"For now, where the fuck else?"

"Then we will have to do it at the hotel beside the consulate."

"Or perhaps we keep changing venues, confirming only at the last minute via some sort of a code . . . keep the originals at the consulate. Take pictures of each page, get those to me, and we take it from there."

"Are you joking?"

"What part of what I said sounded funny?" Shan asked, frowning.

I was surprised not only by her efficiency in plotting how we'd deal with this, but that she offered a new energy, a discipline, to what I'd come to consider a burden.

"Shan, what are the potential consequences?"

"If Zhao disappeared suddenly and sent these to you, then chances are that he was being watched. So we will be careful and hope not to be found out. If we are and you're lucky, you'll be kicked out of China. Sent back home. If you're unlucky and you happen to piss off the wrong person at the wrong time, well, maybe an international incident. For me? The worst scenario, a terrible scenario, is that I would get arrested. A public show of making an example of one considered a *fuerdai*. On the other hand, they may look the other way. Allow it to be published, and then ban it. Or ban it entirely immediately. I don't know. It depends whom it rankles. But, we would have to do this quickly, assiduously."

"What about Arabile?"

"I don't know, Beth. Partly, I wish you hadn't brought this into my life. But now that you have, I cannot unsee it. The kids of the post-revolution have been infinitely distracted with admiring the things our parents were forbidden. We've been coerced into not asking and not speaking, into reading textbooks, all books, to suit a fictitious past. National amnesia! I only learned about Tiananmen when I was studying in the States. And when I came back home and asked my parents about it, they refused to acknowledge that anything like that had occurred. Zhao has written a history, dark and ugly, but real. He brought these papers to you because he knew you wouldn't look away, and in turn you knew that I wouldn't. I don't see that we have a choice. But if we get caught, well. Life will change."

23

CAPE'S CONFESSION

Now I must construct a human being, bit by bit, building her whole from bones, dragged from the grave. Or perhaps liberated, because Kay's grave is in the unloveliest part of Water Falls, amid diseased trees of a species that no one can name any longer, maybe never had a name, that grow now emitting not shade, but shadows. A place where gangs of men roam, on the alert for mourners, dumb with sorrow. How strange I should be the one to free her now.

Limbs: one, two, three . . . here is four. Each slotted in place (should have paid better attention in biology), ribs, pelvis? The other way around, a skull, hair (do hair and nails grow even in death? These will have to be manicured, trimmed). Feet. Her feet, which are unusually long for a seventeen-year-old girl.

The bones I must wrap lovingly in sinew, thick flesh, and a coating of velvety brown skin. In my version, every bit and piece is accounted for. This is how they must see her: far more than child number so-and-so that was killed. The skeleton must be made into something real: a girl, she was only just a girl, with short wild hair and a magical smile. Along with flesh, words must be conjured in what is still only the outline of a story. She was not urban legend, after all, but here—flesh, blood, bones—full warrior. Epic narrative. Saved from historical ephemera, from the place of eternal forgetfulness.

It is Day two; the rest of the first day wasted on clarifying names, spellings, on clearing up any misunderstandings, on tea breaks and a lunch of watery salad and plastic chicken, on the stenographer's desperate search for paper or ink, whatever powers her prose. But really, I think he is stalling for time because he'd like to believe I'm innocent.

Good morning, he says from beneath eyes that try not to dream, did you sleep well? When you are ready to begin, just begin. Say anything you can remember about that day . . . when you found out.

You want me to speak specifically about the day I learned of Kay's death? I ask gently, pinning, as I thought I couldn't, the story to his skin. As Mary Shelley raised the dead, so Kay must be given words, one at a time, to walk her out of that dark, dank place where she has been buried beneath history. What a forgetful nation.

Yes, yes, he says.

I learned from my high school principal, Mr. Salie, that Kay had been killed in a bomb blast. He had been contacted by someone else, I don't know who. Well, I walked out of his office and I suppose I must have been in shock. That's the word.

I wait for the woman behind me, the mouth-breather, to say something, but either she is absent today or has nothing to add. She seems like a regular, there to listen attentively to the ghastly

192

and the macabre for reasons only she knows. I know that my parents are seated somewhere behind me.

The red waxy corridor that led from Mr. Salie's office to my classroom seemed endless that day. Somehow, I collected my bag and perhaps the teacher stopped as I came in, and watched me move across the classroom like the apparition I was to become at that school, but really, I don't remember. I stayed in my room for weeks after that day. At first just trying to get the elemental things back: breathing, eating, sleeping, speaking without crying. To understand what had happened to Kay and how anyone as preternaturally special could die young. When I returned to school, weeks had passed. My friends, if I had ever had any besides Kay, thought of me, saw me, as something different. Untouchable in my sorrow and my politics.

With Kay gone, the student movement in the entire region was at its lowest point. She had been its spine. When I did manage to get back to meetings, into some routine, it was with a specific aim: to find out what had happened to Kay. The truth, you see, was hidden and only the barest of details became known: yes that she was dead; had died from a bomb explosion. No more, and it was left to me to uncover what had truly happened.

And did you?

I learned things, which I am here to tell you.

He looks up sharply. Things which you have written in your submission?

Things which I've not written down, no.

I hear rattling behind me and for a minute think it must be Kay who has come to offer moral support and is just now rearranging the bones that must be so stiff, which must still be relearning the delicate mechanics of movement. I turn for a glimpse, but it is only Ma Mouth-Breather arriving late, shifting a chair so she sits a metre from my right shoulder, jiggling her thick brass bangles. I'm glad to see her and she winks.

Go on, please, he says.

To trace Kay's last movements and activities would require investigation. There was one person I felt might know something about her death: Karl. He was older than us; a conscientious objector who had taken Kay under his wing. Or maybe they were equals, I'm not really sure. Perhaps he knew something beyond rumours, the inadequate police reports, the silence I encountered whenever I asked anyone—teachers, comrades, journalists—what had happened to her. Perhaps he could also explain her vanishings.

Vanishings?

She'd disappear for days at a time. She never let me know when she'd be gone, and even her grandmother was taken by surprise at these times. It happened again right before her death.

Do you know now where she went?

I suspect she was receiving some sort of military training.

Why would you say that, he says, his voice fluttering into the afternoon's stilted air, flying out the window, jolting the Peanut Gallery back to life. I hear them shifting about, fine-tuning for what must surely come.

Whenever she returned from these absences she knew things she hadn't before. There were sudden plans. The way she spoke, like she'd eaten *Das Kapital* for breakfast, lunch, and dinner and was only now bringing up its bones.

Ma Mouth-Breather's quick handclap tells me she likes this. As do the sniggers of my audience.

I mean to say, whenever she reappeared she seemed invigorated; she knew what we should do next and where we should strike.

Strike? He says incredulously.

Well, protest.

Burning tires, he says with a new sourness, as he shakes his head and mumbles something about us having been children.

Perhaps, but sometimes even children must act in their own interests. We weren't inherently violent, none of us. But we knew there were certain things that we had to do if we planned to follow lives of our own choosing . . . acts to achieve freedom, which was the basis of the independence we desired. We understood our parents had given up the fight, which was now ours to continue.

I know my parents hear every word: that my father inspects the shine on his shoes; that my mother chews pale orange lipstick onto her teeth. Like the good Christians they are, they accept their share of guilt for my sins, and I suppose I'm grateful.

Anyway, as distasteful as violence always is, I say, doesn't it have its place? Not only in defence of oneself, one's people, but for justice and equality?

I don't imagine that I have convinced him, or any of his fellow commissioners who look dour, as if I've sullied the memory of an innocent with pragmatism. Perhaps I have.

Go on please, he says coolly.

Karl had started collecting Kay for meetings, to which I wasn't privy. At that point, well, I was an inductee into the ways of the

Struggle and there were things I couldn't know or be told because I might have been a security risk. I wondered if Karl knew something more about her disappearances and her death. Early one morning, I left school on the pretext of having an appointment. Everyone was careful around me, as if *I* had become the time bomb . . . no one objected when I said I'd go see a psychologist at the city's university. I jumped the train there.

You didn't pay? he says, not yet recovered, and I wonder if I've blundered, straying as I have from the story of the hapless victim. But no, she must be made whole with the truth. As must I.

We never paid unless we got caught: our place was at the back of the train in "third class" . . . for black people. We refused their designation by not paying.

Go on, go on . . .

I waited outside the office of the student council the whole afternoon. Everyone knew Karl, had heard about the girl who'd been blown apart. I was ushered into a chair in the corner before being brought cups of tea and sandwiches and promises of the better future that we all, they said, were creating. It was an hour before Karl appeared. And when he did, I almost didn't recognize him. The long yellow locks that once fell around his shoulders had been shorn; there was no sign of unkempt toenails sticking out of DIY sandals; gone was the trippy tie-dyed sweater: suicide vests, we'd called them, because they'd been dyed by one's own hands.

My audience can bear it no longer, and they guffaw openly, hysterically, for almost a minute in agony and relief.

He wore heavy khaki pants, boots and a black T-shirt with the name of a metal band. He was more soldier than student, so the first question I asked was if he'd relented and joined the army.

I have not, he replied. But his heart wasn't in it. In fact, he was not in his own life any longer, it seemed.

How do you mean, my commissioner interrupts.

He was a different person. Not just his clothes, but his mannerisms were different. Gone was the Karl who'd smiled at the rain, spoken with a lilt, replaced by someone who had cracked down the middle. He said he'd wanted to come and find me for so long, but hadn't had the courage.

As we sat outside the student office that day, he said he'd not come to the funeral. Like me, he had not been able to leave his room for weeks. I saw Karl now through the prism of our shared grief.

Did he say anything new?

The last time he'd seen Kay was days before her death. She'd disappeared, as was her habit, but this time, of course, she didn't return. He only knew that something had gone wrong when a comrade called him in the middle of the night telling him about an explosion and talk of a mutilated body found outside Water Falls police station.

A soft sigh escapes Ma Mouth-Breather and I sense her outstretched hand, and my mother's snotty tissue dabbing at her eyes. This can't be easy for them.

By the time my parents collected me from school that day when I'd learned of Kay's murder, a new, even emptier silence had fallen on us. Overlaid by shock and resignation. Theirs. The childish games they'd imagined I occupied myself with, the wild friends, had shaken the peace of their existence. They tried. She brought soup. He sat quietly beside me. Left books on my side table. My father would say towards the end of his life that he'd done the best he could. Maybe so. It just wasn't very much. Instead of finding new ways to bring me closer, they let me go.

Why a bomb? How had the situation come to be, I said, speaking clearly into the microphone. Karl told me he'd heard . . . everyone was speculating . . . that Kay had been trained in ammunitions. That the bombing of the police station was a directive that had gone wrong in her inexperienced hands.

Who ordered this? my commissioner asks.

He thought the movement had, I reply.

He remains very still and I feel his colleagues, the Peanut Gallery, the building itself tilt so that I may whisper into their ears.

I wait them out.

You are saying, testifying, that Kalliope was trained in, among other things, the detonation of bombs, which led to her death?

That was the story. I might have believed it, too. But a few days after I met Karl, I found a letter beneath the wooden flap of my school desk. It said Kay had been killed because the bomb itself, the bomb that she'd been given, was set to explode as soon as she tried to activate it.

The room is silent. Perhaps they've not understood, so I turn around, but from their expressions, my parents' faces, I see that they have followed every word and Ma Mouth-Breather nods encouragingly that I should continue.

Why had I been given this information? But of course, I understood quickly enough that this was a warning to me to refrain from asking any further questions unless I wanted to meet a similar end. In the years since, I . . . well, I'd deduced that the defective bomb must not only have been the doing of the security police, but also of a person so close to Kay—someone compromised—that she'd not even suspected the coming betrayal.

But why murder and not arrest her, my commissioner asks softly.

Why murder children ever? But history is littered with their bodies. The way to damage the student movement while the world was watching—remember who her father was—was to assassinate her but make it appear an accident.

I look up. The man has his chin resting on folded fists, his face more lined than before wearing an expression that wishes to believe in my innocence. Wishes, but doesn't quite. The commissioner beside him concludes the day's events, directing us outside for lunch.

As I reach the exit, a woman like many who attends the sessions each day awaits me. She is hugging a small handbag, her pale grey hands squeezing themselves into knots.

I'm so sorry, she says before I have even reached her. So sorry for your loss . . . for what you endured, and with that she opens her arms and says, I am sorry too because I didn't know what was happening in my own city.

I want to turn away from her, walk out of this place with my make-believe Kay who trails me with her slightly laughable, spasmodic gait. Instead I put my head on the woman's shoulder as she folds me into her perfumed jacket, but I do not permit her to cry with her head buried into my hair as she would like.

24

BENEATH YELLOW MOUNTAIN

By the time I'd circumnavigated the town centre in search of a cup of coffee (I found something black and strong, but cannot say it was coffee), the gang was already at their spot. This time they made way for me. Even the old battle-axe cracked her face and I supposed it would have to do for a smile.

My childhood friend—let us call him Old Lin—looked as if he'd been snatched from the outer edges of life: his last couple of teeth were brown from chewing tobacco, his smile seemed in the process of falling from his face, and his claws were long and dirty. Anyway, he still beat us at mah-jongg. He let out a cry of delight, at least so I interpreted the cackle that sprang from his throat, surprising even him. It was only then that I clearly found him in my memory: the frail boy with the nose that ran like the village stream as he trailed his big sister up and down the narrow lanes trying to sell eggs from the family's chickens.

What happened to that sister of yours? I asked after Old Lin had won three or four games in succession and the gang had dispersed to find lunch or to nag their children and grandchildren.

She left this pigsty decades ago, he said in between slurps of noodle broth, dragging on a cigarette that I had given him. She lives close to the mountain. You can see the yellow mountain with your own eyes from where she lives, can you imagine, he said, jutting his dagger of an elbow into me.

Your whole family survived the great famine?

Oh she was born to survive, that one. But I was her curse to be looked after, he said, again stabbing me with his elbow so I moved out of reach. No, he continued, our parents died and our young brother in '59. My sister saved the two of us.

How did she ensure your survival?

I don't know. Anyway, who cares about old history? No one cares anymore.

I care.

You are probably mad. Anyway, she was a Red Guard, he said with some pride.

Ah, I said. And do you remember what happened to most of the people of this village? The old teacher? That family of boys that loved to sing? I don't recognize anyone at all anymore.

Died.

How?

Famine.

But how come they died from famine?

They ran out of food! he said, as if I must have bumped my head on the road.

Do you remember nothing else? I asked impatiently.

Remember that it is better to forget.

I don't know what became of my mother, I said to him, in a small voice.

Ask my sister. She remembers everything and everyone. Ask her. Maybe she will know.

~

The archives in my home village were at the back of what had once been the Party office. It was a room far smaller than I had imagined, and here as in many other places, all that was needed was for me to show the two women who ran the archives my old press badge and retiree documents.

Come to write a book about this old village? Why? said the sour one, so I was convinced she must be related to old battle-axe.

Don't listen to her! implored the other as she pulled a fistful of peanuts from the pocket of her skirt and fed them into her mouth one at a time as she continued speaking. These old records? No one even looks at them anymore, she said, walking me into a small room that held a metal desk and chair and walls of blue filing cabinets.

You have never read them? I asked, refusing a peanut.

No, why should I, she said, and let a piece of purple shell fall from her fingers to splinter on the floor. But I don't mind if you do, as long as you have permission from higher up, she said, pointing to the heavens.

Correct.

Whatever, she said, and disappeared.

Three days I sat and read—in letters between officials that were perfectly preserved—how my village as well as neighbouring counties had been decimated as hundreds of thousands starved. Let me confess: I wept into my sleeve as I read how my village had been destroyed within two years of the end of 1958 (when I last saw my mother). In that time a quarter of the people had simply disappeared from the records. I saw the same written of neighbouring villages, in letters exchanged in a frenzy among despairing officials. Here: that family of boys, all of them musicians and singers, dead in the space of months. No reason given, so I must conclude that they starved.

And then there was a ghost town.

I was interrupted before I could finish by the peanut-eater, who came bearing a cup of water, drawn from the dispenser I'd seen down the corridor.

What are you still looking at? she asked.

Just a few things, I said, wiping my eyes with the back of my hands.

She peered over my shoulder to read what I'd written.

Burial rites, she read aloud:

- No shallow graves.
- The buried must have crops planted over them.
- All crying prohibited.
- No burials along the road.
- No mourning.

Huh! When was this? she asked.

During the great famine of the late '50s.

Really . . . mmh, well, what could be done? Everyone had to eat bitter then. And look what we have today, hey? A great China. I mean not here, this shit hole is nothing, but . . . anyway, she said, as she left the door ajar and the cup of water on the edge of the desk.

About my mother I could learn nothing: there was no death certificate and I knew, finally, that she could not have stayed behind to mourn and bury Aunty as she had said she would, because the very act of grieving had been outlawed.

Perhaps the mountain air would clear my head.

~

I journeyed for a day to see Old Lin's sister beneath the famous mountain.

But I did not come to visit you, mountain. I did not come to stare at your proud ways (very un-Chinese by the way), as your spirit remains unbowed and unbroken after millennia. I refuse to be moved by the veil of cloud falling between your limbs, or those pine trees crystallized with winter's kiss. I certainly didn't come to stare at you and try my hand at poetry after all these decades. But then I have never before actually seen you. And you should know, the ancient paintings do not do you justice.

But no, these mountain soliloquies must come to an end. There are serious questions to be asked.

After two cups of good strong coffee (they have a nice shop for the tourists that sells decent coffee) and a pack of cigarettes, I found Old Lin's sister's house located in a cove beneath an easterly-facing segment of the mountain. The house (a not-too-ugly reproduction of traditional Chinese architecture) was so close to the mountain that I could trace the outline of every crag, yet it was hidden from the road and this gave it some privacy from the busloads of tourists arriving hourly, unloading their talk and their picture-taking tyranny.

Older sister gave no hint of remembering me, but did not seem to require much information to open the door; just a brother's name. Feng—let us call her this—was not the three-foot menace I remembered, nor did she appear to be the forbidding person Old Lin had described. She was small, with silver flecks in hair cut neck-length, and wore a modern linen take on the Mao suit, and slippers on her petite feet. I was pleased that I had outgrown her.

Come, she invited me into her house, which was not grand, rather the opposite, with almost empty rooms, huge windows that faced the mountain, wooden floors left bare. It was not grand but it was impressive.

Why has my brother sent you to visit me? she asked, as we sat at the long wooden kitchen table, overlooking a courtyard rimed now in frost, but which she said flowered with herbs and multi-coloured chilies during the spring season. She prepared river fish, rice, and spicy soup, which though I was hungry I ate slowly and carefully, as the atmosphere seemed to require.

I wanted to call on you when I heard from your brother that you lived here. He said that perhaps you might tell me more about what happened to our old village.

Did he?

He said your memory was a tiger. I meant to flatter Feng, but could that see she didn't care for praise. He also said you knew a great deal of what happened then, during and after the famine, I added.

Yes, she said, setting her chopsticks down after only a mouthful or two. There is much that I do recall, but why would I want to?

Why not? Is our modern China not founded on whatever came before this moment? I asked, repeating the words I had often heard spoken.

She looked at me for a long time before she replied, her thick silver ring clinking on the cup that held her tea, her eyes never wavering from my face.

It seems to me you are trying to catch a fish by climbing a tree. No, you have not come all this way to see someone that you hardly even liked, nor to repeat a few well-worn phrases. I suggest you speak plainly; we are getting older every second.

My mother disappeared, I said then. My Aunty died of starvation. The past is my living nightmare and I want answers.

I remember them both. They were clever women.

Yes, I replied warmly.

Your Aunty died very early in the famine.

But was it just a famine, after all?

Of course not.

What was it?

It was the beginning of all of this—like you said—this new country of ours. She pointed to a world beyond. And also, the machinations of a new power.

Your brother told me that you buried your parents, a younger sibling during that famine. How did they die?

They starved.

I waited for her to continue, but for a long time she said nothing and all we heard was the wind shifting through the trees.

Tell me, she said after perhaps ten minutes had passed, have you ever murdered a man?

But of course not.

In all these years, only my brother and I have known what it took for us to survive. You see, I was responsible for him. He says that he was my burden; true, still is. When I was only five my mother placed him in my arms and said I was to care for him as if he were my own. She had to return to the fields. And so he became mine to care for. By the time she had another child, well, things had changed in China. And she loved that new baby the way she didn't, or could not, love either of us. I tell you this, she said, tracing the wooden table with her ringed finger, because what I will say next I have never told anyone. I have never spoken these words. But then, no one in all these decades has ever asked me the questions that you have. And so, nearing the end of my life, I am finally provided with the opportunity to ease my conscience. I offer you a deal: I wish to free myself, but if I do so, then you become imprisoned.

Yes, I said, acceding to I knew not what.

We ate my parents.

I was astonished at her words, thought it a terrible moment for a joke, but when I looked at her face, I understood that she was entirely serious.

My parents died of starvation. And when they were still freshly dead, we cooked and ate them with the few cooking utensils we could scavenge. Perhaps it was two weeks later that we ate our younger brother who was so weak, he was not conscious when I put the blanket over his face. It required a grave, terrible act on my part. She pushed her food away from her.

Have you ever been hungry? Starving? There is no line between what you will and will not do, she said. Only the hunger speaks, screams in tongues, so conscience, morality, right, wrong—these are just words born from empty ideas. Only an empty stomach sets rules.

She did not speak for a very long time. And then slowly resumed:

We had no choice, she said, as her finger persisted in tracing the arcs and impressions of the table. A few months after your Aunty died, there was no food left in our village: we'd eaten everything. Not even a mouse was left to wander about. The communes were empty of even one grain of wheat; we had been abandoned by the very people who had come to save us. This was how it was across our village and many more, I heard. The great taboo in cultures that came far before and certainly after ours— against eating whatever you must to survive—got crossed again and again on the path to survival. And if my brother and I were to escape our village alive, before we became someone else's meal, then we needed strength. And so we succumbed to nature's vilest impulses. If this is life—after what was done to ensure our survival—then yes, we are alive.

She stood up and walked towards a window that faced a wall of rock.

I pushed the food away, stood and made my way towards the door on tremulous legs.

Your mother, she called before I reached for the handle, was not among the dead in our village. She left for the county seat, where she said she had people who could do something about what was happening to us. That she'd be back, but I never saw her again.

I opened the door and walked away.

25

THE AMERICAN HOUSE

Back in Harlem.

Tired.

Weary.

Man, I think I am the blues.

A couple of letters here before me. Two. Addressed to you. I walked late yesterday all the way downtown with these in my jacket pocket. That's where I keep them safe. How I kept them all the way from Carmel. Where they never leave. I think I will post them today, adding this new one to the pile.

Lord knows your letters to me grow more insistent each day, asking what it is you have done wrong and why I have abandoned you.

I think you are guilty of kindness. Of attention.

Maybe today I will overcome the worry of what you will say when you understand what my survival has demanded. Yesterday I tried, but couldn't bring myself to push the letters through the slot. Maybe today. May be.

~

I offer you advice: be careful of this writing life. It will devour you from within and perhaps from without too.

It's been weeks now since I sat before (and beneath) the judgment of other men. I am not a communist, I said. Now I hold an ear to the ground (chatter rises from friends and foes alike) and I hear it all right: liar, turncoat, coward. But these are greater lies.

Apostate?

Me?

Who said that?

No, I am a reasonable man. A man who has spent all his life as a literary sharecropper, selling my word. Hustling between reading and speaking gigs, operettas, children's books, plays, musicals—all so I could survive in the life that I chose. I am a man who knows what it means to be "cullud" in the world. It means this: Hold your head down when you need to.

~

I'd written *Goodbye Christ* when first I'd left these United States in the early 1930s and out there seemed to find a world less concerned, less troubled, by the colour of my skin. It was near a decade later, as I was about to embark on a tour to promote my newly published autobiography *The Big Sea* (still hot in my hands from the printing press), when that damn poem resounded in ways I did not expect. People who walked with their hands on their bibles, a song in their heart and a murderous glint in their eyes unearthed the verse, and sought to undo all I had accomplished. Man, it got ugly. Protests and picket lines instead of audiences and fans! Heaps of letters and articles saying I had turned my back on my God-fearing people! For days, weeks, and months I could not open a newspaper, letter, or wire (they arrived by the dozen) asking what in blazes I had meant by that poem, while others admonished me for ever having written it. For weeks I got out of bed each day, before settling right back in, hoping it would all soon blow over. It did not. The poet had his national acclaim, but not the way he had wanted.

Perhaps now you will say: Langston—but did you mean it, the words in *Goodbye Christ*?

Answer: but have I not repudiated that question already?

You see, friend, I had (unwittingly) swung at the heart of my people's beliefs. I could not stay in their favor if I continued in that line (and their agreement, as you know by now, was what my life's work had been about). Then, as I would again at the Senate trials, I rejected the poem as a foolishness of youth. Guess it was true too. What right-thinking cullud poet, who writes of the struggles of the Negro but must rely on the generosity of the white man to publish his wanderings, thinks he has the right to speak free? To think and do as he likes? Only a madman!

Was this the reason for my calling before the American people? Yes. And yet, there is something else which I must tell you.

You will recall that back in 1933 I had visited Japan on my way to China. The trip home from Shanghai would take me back to Japan. And it was here that something happened when I stopped in Tokyo, which informs the present, some decades later. Tokyo: the city in which I had been so warmly welcomed and honored before, would now unceremoniously expel me like a common thief!

Once the boat had dropped anchor, I checked into a hotel. Tired to my bones, I was looking forward to dinner and perhaps a movie when I was called down to the lobby. There stood a few burly men, whom I did not recognize as writers though they identified themselves as such.

R: They did not look like writers?

L: Why, no. But then, you did not imagine from my photos that I was a writer—too proper (and perhaps well-fed) rather than bohemian, you said.

R: You sound offended?

L: I may as well say that, yes, I was.

R: But come now, how could I—a minor writer—offend a great international writer like yourself?

But now, let me finish this story so that I may attend to the pile of manuscripts and letters threatening to crash into my ceiling. (Are these imagined conversations better kept to myself? I would not continue had *you* not encouraged me in previous letters.)

The two men, after questioning me for a while in the lobby, dropped the game and openly invited me to Tokyo Metro Police Station for further interrogation.

"Why were you in Shanghai?" the larger of the two men asked once we were seated.

"I had never before visited that city, that country, and I was curious to see it as any tourist might," I answered.

"What did you see?"

"Why, I walked along the Bund many an afternoon. I visited the city's many beautiful parks. I listened to jazz and such stuff. Things a tourist might normally do."

"You left the international concessions?"

"When occasion demanded it."

214

"And when did occasion demand it?" the smaller man, who until this point had been silent, asked in a menacing tone.

"When I wanted to explore the whole city."

He stood up then, spoke rapidly in Japanese to the other man, so I understood he was in charge. A fact he cared to have me know then.

"When did you leave the concessions and where did you go?" he demanded this time, bearing down on me.

"Gentlemen," I replied, "your invitation has run its course and I now would like to see the American consul in this city."

"In due course," said the larger man.

"No, now," said I.

"Later," said he.

"Am I to understand then that I am detained?"

"No, you are our guest."

"And yet your guest is not free to leave, is that so?"

"You will be free to leave as soon as you have told us what we wish to know."

"What do you wish to know?" said I, my hands trembling. With anguish, and yes, fear too, for those were tumultuous times. The world then felt as if it were swinging, ready any moment to catapult into something new, or, to be yanked back into the old. Depending on what I said, I imagined my fate to be as perilous.

"Why did you visit the offices of a communist magazine?"

"To see a friend of a friend."

"This friend of a friend, do you know he is a communist?"

"No, I am not in the habit of asking my friends' friends for their political affiliations before I have even met them."

"Do you know that the friend you speak of, that you dined with regularly in Moscow, has been instrumental in organizing a communist cell—a spy network, Mr. Hughes—that stretches from Moscow to Shanghai to Tokyo to the Western world," he said pounding the desk with a tight fist as he named each place. "And this network threatens to destabilize the entire region, maybe the whole world? Now is it coincidence that your friendly visits coincide exactly with the people and places of this spy network?"

"I know nothing of what you say. My friend is a writer! An American! I very much doubt she could be as influential as you say," I said, my palms hot and sticky, my collar feeling like a noose around my neck.

"And why visit Madame Sun Yat-sen?" said the larger man.

"She invited me to dinner."

"Why did she invite you to dinner?" he replied convivially, as if we were right that moment sitting on a balcony sipping bourbon and shooting the breeze.

"She had read some of my poetry and had liked it. But say, given the chance, would you not wish to pay your respects to a founding parent of your own, or anyone else's, country?"

"What did you talk about?" asked the more aggressive man.

"Ballet. And books. Writers, these sorts of things."

"Did you speak about your friend in Moscow or about the Madame's socialist sympathies? Did she give you anything: a note? A letter? A message?"

"No."

"Madame Sun Yat-sen knows your friend in Moscow very well." A statement.

"I do not know."

"Mr. Hughes," began the smaller one, again bearing down on me and flashing some ragged incisors: "Are you a communist?"

"I have never joined a political party, as I fear it would compromise my independence of thought and the ability to remain critical in general."

"Did you carry messages from your friend in Moscow to Madame Sun Yat-sen and others that you met, like the communist writer Lu Hsun? Or the editor of that communist journal that you visited?" his voice was fierce and must have echoed well beyond that room.

"You have already asked. I did not. Am I now free to go?"

"No."

"Are you a communist?"

"I have answered that question already."

"Not satisfactorily, and until you do, we will not release you."

"So, am I to understand that I am a prisoner of the Japanese government?"

"No, you are our guest," said the larger man.

"Answer!" said the shorter man.

"I am not, nor have I ever been, a communist."

"But your poems—here, full of communistic messaging," said the good cop, rifling through a stack of papers that I came to understand then were in fact my poems.

"I write about freedom. For my own people. For all subjugated peoples."

"Like the Chinese?"

"You said it."

"So you imagine the Chinese are oppressed like Negroes?" said the bad cop.

"Are they not? Are you not an occupying force?"

"No more than your own country."

"Well, I do not always agree with my own country," I began to say, and too late decided against it.

"How so?" Good cop.

"In my own country I am a Negro. A title I bear with pride, yet I am not allowed into certain places in certain states. Some people cross to the other side of the road when they see me coming, as if I am contaminated, as if my skin is a disease rather than a beautiful shade of black. In short, in my own country, I am a second-class citizen."

"And you and your friends believe communism will overthrow oppression of the brown, black and yellow people of the world if they unite?" asked the larger man. Despite his tone, panic flew from my head to my fingers, which started to tap against the wooden table. Was it coincidence that the man echoed a poem I had just written on the boat journey from Shanghai to Tokyo, and which I had thought safe beneath the carpet of my room?

"I have already answered your questions about communism. I will say no more."

On and on hour after hour the interrogation continued. There was no respite, only a measly offering of an American hamburger and some tea that marked lunchtime. But the questions, the interrogations, the scarcely veiled threats (no one knew where I was) did not abate until I had been there for more than

218

twenty-four hours. And only then was I finally released and deported like a common criminal.

After that I got back home and my troubles mounted still! I fell ill around then too and for weeks I lay in a hospital bed, delirious and in misery. I was sick, maligned and broke, my troubles growing by the day. Even the holes in my pockets had holes in them. I could not pay my rent in Harlem and I was duly evicted. Man, I had no career, no money, fewer friends and no home. And someone had dared to call me the Poet Laureate of Harlem!

If I hadn't known it before, I was reminded now that the Negro writer who wants to eat (or write) needs to make a choice. Say what you like: you're broke. Live how you want: you're broke and no friends. Now, what choice you mean? I learned my lesson.

So when Senator McCarthy called me to answer, was there some idea of a report—a dossier—compiled decades before? Was this, and that damned poem, the basis of my latest persecution?

You ask finally: was that true then, Langston? You never truly believed in communism and you did not aid the revolutionaries when you visited Shanghai in the summer of '33?

I have answered your question.

Anyway, what is this truth you keep hammering on about? Look to my life's work. There you will find answers, words woven into truths.

But now I must go. I have these letters—three—burning a hole in my pocket and they are destined for you. L

26

THE SHANGHAI BOOK CLUB

Unfamiliar sounds woke me every night, and one evening so convinced was I that someone had broken in, I hid beneath the guestroom bed to listen to a repetitive clawing and what sounded like the distant echo of feet. Even after the sounds died down I stayed under the bed, immobilized by my fear. I fell asleep and awoke an hour or two later into the usual Shanghai cacophony, stiff and ashamed. I found nothing amiss as I walked through the apartment, a can of mace in my hand. Only when I reached the kitchen did I catch a foreign scent that had been left there to linger. Someone had been in my place as I'd slept; had fiddled with the lock on the kitchen door and left it ajar.

On the counter was an envelope like the ones I'd first received from Zhao. Inside it were more papers: letters, I guessed, which bore dates: two months ago, one month, two weeks, and one written only days earlier.

~

Shan's instructions and labour were assiduous, constant, no matter how much of Zhao's writing I threw at her. Her first order was that I take pictures of every page Zhao had sent. She'd tucked a phone into an envelope to be used for this purpose, which Arabile left wordlessly on my desk. I was to return the phone the very next day, so the entire night was spent taking pictures of Zhao's scribbles or typing. The manuscript amounted to hundreds of pages, some illegible, so I understood the enormity of Shan's task, and didn't think it right to complain that I wouldn't get any sleep that night. From the photos of the manuscript, she created a new chapter almost every evening, saved it on a memory stick, and had it placed on my desk the next day.

How to come to know a man, first in person and then again, more thoroughly, by his written admissions? Nights came to mean something new yet again (I saw Kamal every few evenings and sometimes gave up this work to be with him).

But I was consumed with the waiting, the reading, the search for a word or phrase. As Shan was careful with Zhao's writing, so was I with her translation, adding a flourish as I reckoned Zhao might, or finishing a line so I could put his spirit into the text.

How I missed him, I could finally admit. How I missed Kay too. How their friendships had broken and shaped me. Reshaped me in the breaking, maybe as rare friendships do. The sense that I was no longer doing this for myself became clear and compelling. I traded sleep for editing, and in the cold early hours I understood the details of Zhao's telling had been too intense to be passed per mouth, his confessions too shocking to be received eye to eye. No, never to be spoken. ⟵ audience

Arabile arrived at work every morning with a brown envelope, which he dropped on my desk without saying a word. He no longer sought me out or chatted when we passed each other in the passageway. He carried the sense of a man who'd been compelled into a folly, as if we'd persuaded him to go on a picnic in the rain, when really, we all now understood that the rest of our lives could depend on this moment.

~

As chilly days gave way to lengthy warm evenings and even warmer days, colour began to drift up from the garden: first shades of blue and violet, trees returning to emerald life, until a blur of yellow erupted throughout. Still, Shanghai remained beneath a dishwater sky. Shan and I worked every evening, meeting up once a week, always in new locations, to go over what she'd found.

"I threw the phone across the room," she said. "He was there, had seen everything, but did what?"

"That phone is our record. Anyway, what could he have done?" I said.

"Something more, Beth, something more than just record history."

"A history that would have been lost if it were not for people like Zhao. However late."

Shan gave me another set of instructions at that lunch that I'd appreciate fully in days to come. Now that we were nearing the end of the project, I was to email all the pages we'd amassed, all the ones I had already typed, all the pictures of the manuscript I'd taken, all that she had translated and that I'd corrected to someone outside of China. She repeated what she'd said early on in our collaboration: that no one, not Kamal or anyone else on Chinese soil, should know what we were doing.

I set up a virtual private network in the USA from the personal laptop that I hardly ever used, created a new email address, and called Andrew from my mobile phone.

"Beth? What time is it? Are you all right?" It was as if I could see him, fully dressed and fast asleep on the couch in front of the television, feeling around for his watch. On the rug in front of you, I wanted to say but didn't.

"I'm sorry to call so late . . . Andrew, but I have something really important to ask of you."

"What is it, Beth? " he said, without hesitation.

"I emailed you some documents. You need to print them and hold onto them for me," I said, a soft urgency in my voice that I hoped he remembered and for which he still had a vestige of love.

"Are you all right?" his voice turned to steel.

"I'm fine."

"Then . . ." he said.

"Did you sign the papers," I asked, quickly changing the subject.

"No, not yet . . ."

"But you will of course?"

"Yes, if that's what you want. If you want to end our marriage, Beth?"

"You're asking the wrong questions, Andrew."

"Shit, Beth. The way you just left. You didn't even let us speak about it. You transferred so fast to China there was no chance to try to work things out, get counselling . . . and then a letter from a law firm a few weeks back, after barely any word from you this entire year. Not one phone call returned—now you ask for a favour at midnight and if I signed the divorce papers?" he said, so rapidly that I knew he was trying to get it all in before I disappeared again.

"You don't believe in therapy," I said, incredulously. "Anyway, it was hard to get a word in with your constant hectoring."

"Hectoring trumps collaboration."

"Ah, because you did everything right? You know, I believed you to be a man above reproach. At least I could hold onto that knowledge as everything else started to slip: your solid ethics, your contempt for the corrupt and those who trampled on others. Your honesty. But that didn't quite apply to me, did it, Andrew?"

He went quiet.

"You were so obvious, Andrew. I knew you; always had. Maybe somewhere along the way we stopped speaking honestly to each other: stopped being us, but I still knew you. The way you moved, when you were avoiding me. And then someone, your old legal partner actually, who hated how you'd turned against government, called to tell me that she saw you having lunch too often, she said, with a blonde lady. I couldn't bear to ask you if it was true because then, truly, what was there left to believe in?

"Beth. I'm sorry. It wasn't what you think it was . . . I mean it was, I . . . things happened," he said so softly I had to hold the phone tighter to my ear, and his words pierced the soft flesh I'd been trying to grow a layer around. "But I didn't stop loving you. I don't think that's possible . . . I was so tired of the pretence, of who you'd become."

"Don't, Andrew . . ."

"Why not? What rule am I breaching now? I didn't speak ill or, fuck, ever, about the dead. Then I wasn't allowed to speak about your work, your corrupt colleagues, or about the 1980s . . ."

"Speaking? You were always lecturing me, haranguing me, really, about my choices, my conscience, as if I didn't carry the weight of my own decisions. At least I was faithful to you." He was so quiet I couldn't even hear the thin nose whistle he'd had since a botched operation on his sinuses.

"God, Andrew, on top of the betrayal, is the humiliation. If your old colleague knew . . . you couldn't even leave me my pride? And then, well, I was stunned. Thought you'd had a weakness for brown exotics only, not strawberry blondes."

His breath shuddered down the line.

"Jesus, Beth. That was incredibly low of you to say. But you couldn't have raised it? Raised hell? Asked me why? No . . . you just slunk away like you've always done."

"You might have denied it, or worse, admitted to it."

"Our marriage had been more wonderful than not, Beth," he said.

"It doesn't matter any longer . . . I didn't call about this."

"It does matter. Greatly. You betrayed me too, Beth, when you changed your values. Became all right with complicity. Someone able to capitulate to being part of a dysfunctional and corrupt government. That was never who you were or who we were when we came together. You changed the alchemy. And it was like you were living in hiding. In plain sight, but virtually unseen. So somewhere along the line, you also broke a bond."

226

"Oh, wait: you are blaming me for your cheating," I said, under a curdled laugh.

"No, of course not. I am so sorry, Beth. Getting into it with . . . with her . . ."

"Who?"

"A doctor I met when we were suing about the state of public hospitals."

"How noble."

"It was stupid. A distraction for me and her."

"Cruel?"

"Yes, cruel. Hurtful. And I'm paying the price here. Just seemed we were on different sides and slipping away came easily. You were choosing all of that, them, over us and we were going in different directions. I lost you, Beth. And you acted like you were sleeping with the enemy."

"It was more complicated than that, Andrew."

"Was it? When you were exposed to corruption, as you must have been many times—but no longer said anything to me about it—did you at least report it? Whistle-blow? Send it anonymously to the papers?"

"You wanted me to turn on my comrades? Former colleagues? And how could I tell you? You were . . ."

"What? The enemy? Beth, I wanted you to report those who were stealing resources that belonged to us, the country, the people, Beth. Who were bit by bit undoing all our lives. That was our contract with the country . . . with the people. The courage required of a civil servant; that's what I needed from you. What you would have demanded of yourself once. Weren't you the girl who walked into a room and placed yourself in front of the whole country to be judged? To hold us all up to scrutiny? For everyone to account . . ."

"Oh Andrew . . . but that didn't work out so well for me."

"Because you lost your nerve."

"Because testifying took my last bit of courage. I did it for Kay, because they forgot about her in the larger scheme of things. And for myself, so I'd finally be released from the guilt, memories, dreams . . . I wanted a normal life in a free country. With you."

"There's no such thing as a normal life if it means complicity, Beth. Anyway . . . I would have tried therapy. Should have gone with you."

Of course, he was right, but I didn't say it.

"It's too late now, Andrew."

He went silent for a long while, until eventually I spoke.

"You'll print those documents now?"

"Now?"

"Yes, it's about the house . . ." I said, feeling foolish, as much over the fact that I'd just revealed my plumbing, my viscera actually, to one of the ever-present Chinese censors somewhere. If Zhao's friend, or whoever my nocturnal visitor had been, was able to penetrate my world so easily, then what of a government that employed thousands, perhaps millions of people to monitor and listen to phone calls, read emails and social media postings, however trivial, sordid, or horrid? "I'll be in touch," I said, and rang off.

I stopped taking the train to work around then. The endless stream of bodies that pushed onto the Metro had been cultural cold water at first, plunging me, it seemed, straight into the city's excesses. But the odd encounters with strangers had ended any enjoyment of the escapade. I only used taxis now. That morning, a few days after I'd called Andrew, was no different.

I had barely walked into my office when Arabile walked in behind me.

"Let's get a coffee," he said, and indicated that I should follow him out of the building.

"Do you have a phone on you?" he asked, once we were walking towards the Bund.

"No, I left it behind."

"Shan believes she was followed last night. Someone walked behind her as she left work. Seemed to track her in a car, and then walked behind her for some ten minutes. This morning she is terrified. No, I am terrified, and furious that you brought her into this," Arabile said, stopping to look at me. "Why did you do this?"

"I didn't realize what would be in those manuscripts, Arabile. I had some notion, but no idea of the scale. I needed someone and Shan was interested. But maybe you're right, perhaps it was a mistake to bring anyone else into this." He was immovable.

"But tell me," I tried, "what would you have done if a friend that you had come to care for . . . to love . . . had suddenly disappeared? Then started sending you, *you*, writings and letters that seemed written to make sense of a past that he'd not even once spoken about? Would you abandon that, him?"

"For fuck's sake," he said. I'd never heard Arabile curse and the effect unnerved me. "This is China. You are a goddamn consul, as am I. We could get arrested. Worse. Disappeared. Disavowed. But that doesn't even touch on what could happen to Shan. Do you know what you've done to our lives?"

"Arabile, Shan made her own decision about what to do. I gave her the option to walk away. She still could. This is my burden. You two walk away from it and I'll face whatever happens next."

"What? You're brave? Or you're naïve? What are you playing at? Look at what you do for a living and now suddenly you want to be a hero? You're a fucking civil servant for an ever more corrupt government. Sure, I work for the same institution, but at least my decision was pragmatic, and you can tell that bunch of gossip-mongers you call a consular staff this too: I took this job, for which I am overqualified, so I could be with my wife in a city that veers between loving and loathing me. All I want is anonymity, that's who I am right? What do I get instead? Fantasies that vary between NBA hero and criminal. Still, I choose love. Every day. But you and your cohort? Your decision is what? Ideological? Or worse, you're a post-ideological civil servant trying to make right with yourself after years of ignoring spiralling ineptitude and corruption?" he said, so furious I could hear his breathe quaking beneath his chest.

"Walk away, Arabile. You and Shan walk away." He spun on his heel and left me standing on the sidewalk.

Arabile's words shattered me the way a gentle man's words might. The way Andrew's had days earlier. Maybe they had found a place of truth. After all, how many decades had I run from my conscience, finding distraction in daily work, in bureaucracy and setting small matters right, when in reality I was part of a failing project: a government that I knew had largely given up on the collective dream of a society that was supposed to have been better, done better. Our dream had died beneath the weight of greed, expediency, nepotism, dishonesty. Maybe Andrew was right: my first-class seat meant I wasn't merely an observer, as I liked to believe, but a participant. Now in one fell swoop I'd tried to correct my own path, mollify my conscience by doing something valiant. Yes, it was the right thing, but I had ruined two, probably three perfectly good lives.

That night I took the papers from the consulate, placed them in a bag and walked to the train station, where I caught a bus. I got off two blocks from my apartment and walked a zigzag pattern home. I emailed Andrew the final pages, barely reading them, before I stomped on the phone until it was cartoonishly wrecked. I submerged its entrails in a bowl of water, turned off the lights, disabled the smoke detectors, opened the windows as wide as they could go on a high floor, and burned Zhao's pages one by one in the kitchen sink. All the while saying a silent prayer that Andrew had already received and printed everything.

27

CAPE'S CONFESSION

Ink flings free from newspaper headlines as posters moored to electricity poles run the length of the road:

Dead Girl's Story Drama.

Despite the obviousness of it all, it is only as we near the hall and see the huddle of reporters at the entrance, the queue of people wrapping the building, that it occurs to me and Kay that she is in fact the dead girl, and I her storyteller.

Kay, whom I've resurrected, sits mutely as we pull into the parking lot. I suspect she's not yet remembered the power of speech, or worked out how to coordinate jaw, tongue, lips, throat. I'd read once that relearning speech is an arduous task, that it can take stroke patients months and years of practice to relearn the mechanics of it. ⌒ a collective ⌒ history

Kay's story, our story, is a sensation. A reporter sits each day in the gallery, diligently noting my words.

The witness insists on a complex portrayal of her friend, who was not only killed, but allegedly betrayed, when she was given a defective limpet mine.

She sees Kay. But does she see me yet?

We make our way into the hall via a side entrance that I have only passed before, yet now we slip through the space held ajar by a broken brick and walk the passageway.

As I enter the room I run my eyes along the rows: it is early and only a handful of staff hover. My parents are not yet in their usual place. Before I have reached the front row I see her and my limbs become useless with shock. They are heavy, too heavy to move.

It is Kay, as I live and have temporarily ceased to breathe.

Kay with living years stitched onto her.

She would have been twenty-five if she'd survived and I make the odd realization then that I have never before thought of the woman Kay would become, only the girl she was. Yet, there she sits, no, here, here before me, poised and dressed in black slacks and high heels and a dark grey V-necked jersey. Elegant and bony, but not so bony that she's a corpse. Her hair is no longer short, but down to her shoulders, unnaturally straight in a long pageboy. I wonder how she has jumped ahead of me when she was behind me a second ago in the passageway. After all, I know the necessity of keeping my mind fixed on Kay as if she were a living person, so that the audience, the reporters and especially him, my commissioner, will see a Kay-shaped space, emptied of life, rather than just a dead girl.

Kay stands, stares right back. And then starts walking slowly towards me. I am terrified, petrified, that I have finally lost my mind because no longer do I wilfully imagine the dead come to life but I do so now involuntarily. The ghost that I've forced myself to create, speak to, to hold me steady has materialized, assumed a life of its own, at least in my head. I am not so mad yet that I don't know that I'm hallucinating.

You're pale, she says urgently, rushing over as my knees give way like a starlet in a black-and-white flick, so the balcony where reporters are still setting up stirs to life, heads shooting over the polished wooden railings one by one.

Help me, Kay calls to the guard watching the scene unfold from her post at the back of the room. I think she's in shock, she says. Through the distance I hear her say, I'm Lucie, Kay's mummy.

When I manage to sit up she says again, I'm her mummy, Lucie. It's because we look so much alike? How stupid of me to forget how much alike we looked. People used to say we could be sisters. But of course I was eighteen years older. I should have let you know I was coming, she says, and sends the guard to fetch sweet tea.

They fuss and fan me. Push a huge chipped mug that says "The truth will set you free" into my hands and speak to me as if I'm a child. It takes a while before I reply.

Kay used to speak about you . . . all the time. How smart you were, how tough . . . but I had no idea how much alike you looked; photos didn't do the resemblance justice.

But now that I look closely, I see that it isn't Kay after all. Certainly her likeness with a few extra lines, but not Kay at all, especially the hair, which has been blow-dried into obedience. Kay didn't own a hairbrush.

At first I wasn't sure I could come here and listen, she says. People said in the beginning, I think maybe you know this, they said that it was you who gave her up to the police. But when I started reading the newspapers in the last week and read what you were saying about Kay, I thought maybe it was time to listen to you. She flicks her head to the side with the confidence of a woman often admired. People love to skinner, even about someone else's dead child, she says, swallowing the offensive word quickly. I thought, let me come. It's clear that you loved her, that I should give you the benefit of the doubt. The things you say, well, proud, I feel proud. So here I am to listen to Kay's best friend, she says as she swipes at tears running down her face. Seven years . . . you never get over a child.

When everyone is seated, the old hall, packed with the curious, the morose, and the professional snoops alike, returns to its purpose. I look back. Lucie smiles encouragingly, as does Ma Mouth-Breather. My mother offers a wave that comes off as regal; a mad queen acknowledging a long-forgotten subject. People stack up against the once-white walls. The gallery so full, reporters stand on the stairwell. They have come to hear me speak about Kay because word has spread about the plot twists, the intrigue and shifting form of my tale. I know I must keep them interested till the very end, pushing back the order to execute.

I am calmer now, but my hands still tremble and I can see that my commissioner watches me closely.

Please begin, he says.

I wasn't dissuaded from looking for answers about Kay's death by the note that had been left for me at school. I called Kay's grandmother, but by then she wouldn't take my calls: blame had been allocated. The opportunistic low-order rat had been found. Still, I asked all the questions that needed to be asked.

Did you try to enrol anyone else in this quest of yours? Your comrades, perhaps? he asks.

I was sidelined, or at least no one kept me informed any longer. Only a campaign of whispers remained. When I stopped long enough to listen, the voices said that I was responsible for Kay's death and my own isolation.

What did you learn from your investigations?

I am getting to it, I say. I am not yet ready. They, my commissioner and the Peanut Gallery, are not ready.

During this time, Sammy Jacobs—Kay's one-time neighbour—was one of a handful that didn't avoid me. At school I was unapproachable, in politics untouchable, and Sammy's attention was a small mercy. He believed me. I had changed but then so had Sammy.

How so?

Well, for starters, he no longer held together the street corners with button heads, dropouts, and gun runners smoking Mandrax and dagga. He said Kay's death had changed him and he no longer wanted to be a letdown to his mother, or anyone else around him. He cleaned up, got a job packing boxes. He said it was a place to start. He began to dress better, eat better, and many days I couldn't breathe for the amount of perfume he wore. Sammy even got a small scooter and on his day off would collect me from school, so I'd sit on the back clinging to him, as we wove home amid the traffic. The change didn't strike me as odd. Not at first. I wanted to believe that I'd had an effect on him, too.

I crack a pause into the stilted air, counting to five for drama before continuing.

One day Sammy invited me to visit him at home, right next door to where Kay had lived. Kay's grandmother had gone to live with her daughter in Johannesburg by then, I say, and catch a toss of Lucie's hair in my peripheral vision. Their house had been rented to another family.

Sammy's house was impeccable and I was struck by how new everything seemed: cream linen curtains that ran the length of the walls, a modern television set topped with a cheerful posy of nylon flowers. In the kitchen the appliances shone; newly opened boxes lined the tops of the cupboards. Of course, no one in Water Falls could afford whimsy like this, never mind on a packer's salary.

Until then, Sammy had always behaved in a way that was, back then, called gentlemanly. But really, I was a child and he an adult. Aside from once when he'd tried to kiss me and I'd rebuffed him, he had respected my wishes. And so on the day when he invited me to see his bedroom I understood it as an invitation to see, well, his bedroom.

A man starts to chuckle. Perhaps it is Ma Mouth-Breather or Lucie who stares him down until he whimpers a limp apology.

His room was a shock to me: red satiny curtains and a double bed laid with frilly cushions in increasingly vulgar shades of red, yellow, and purple, so the bedroom felt like a shrine to, well, not sleep.

There is utter silence in the hall.

"I made this for you," he said, gesturing to the scene around us. In the few seconds which it had taken to step from the lounge

238

into his bedroom, the earth had turned for me and Sammy. There was an unspoken expectation. His. I could feel it breathing on my back, crawling up my legs. To buy time, I walked to his record collection: not one album by Prince. In fact, nothing of interest aside from an old Pink Floyd album which I immediately assumed he'd stolen.

He must have forgotten about the book, but I noticed the small hardback almost immediately: its neat, square handwriting that I knew, had known so well from all the messages that had been written for me in that hand. Kay's journal had been a vanity she'd maintained: writing in the book each day, despite the fear that if it fell into the wrong hands, well, it would have led to her arrest or far worse. My eyes made the calculation. Sammy's window was less than a metre from what had been Kay's bedroom. How tightly the houses were packed together. I imagined Sammy's arm stretching through the open window and into the sanctity of her bedroom. Why had Kay not hidden it better? I evaluated the pristine new furniture and appliances and I wondered.

You suspected Sammy of being a paid informant?, my commissioner asks harshly, losing patience with me.

In that moment I suspected that, yes, he had been paid to inform on Kay. The police made regular swoops for drugs, guns, preemptive arrests, bribes, favours. What if Sammy made a bargain with the devil and said, There is a terrorist living right outside my window? It would have been easy enough for him to get someone to plant the note beneath my school desk.

I don't really know what happened next: he pulled me at first gently, then more forcefully to the bed, insisting all the while that he had been so patient; that he could have asked anytime before, even that night as I walked home alone, but he'd waited and been patient and done all of this so it would be proper, now why was I being a cold fish? Why was I seeming so unwilling? Was it because he was from the Skriwe Flats? Wasn't he good enough for me? Was I a madam and not a comrade after all? He held me under as his garbled words became a steady wet stream in my ear. I lay very very still. I didn't say no. I tried to. Was he right: Was I just a middle-class brat and not a revolutionary . . . who wanted his attention, his affections, without giving back a single thing? Shame slunk over me.

I leave a hollow in the day, to be filled by their terrible thoughts, by my audience's worst, most accurate fears. I sense my parents during every second, their fluttering stuttering hearts.

It was sometime later that I heard his mother arriving home. Distracted, he loosened is grip on my arm, released the nub of his elbow from where it had been ground into my clavicle.

Rage exploded from me then, from my legs and arms and I landed a blow that doubled him over. Free, I ran, fled that room and that house, stopping only when I was shut inside my bedroom.

The room is still. My commissioner doesn't ask whether I would like to adjourn for the day. He simply rises and leaves the hall. My mother is weeping as I pass her. My father looks up, meets me eye to eye. That's not the end of it yet, I say with the briefest glimpse.

Lucie is standing at the door as I knew she would be. She pulls me into her, so tightly that her V-neck sweater tickles my cheek. We do not cry.

28

BENEATH YELLOW MOUNTAIN

The county seat had become a thriving city. Here my mother had come, Feng said.

I suppose these old legs must have walked me onto a train that took me from the mountainous paradise to here, arriving some eight hours later with punched tickets in my hands as proof of my journey? If so, then I must have been in a coma. Or drunk (a real possibility). Or perhaps it was my uninvited city guests—the ones who had started to pay me regular visits, which led to my taking flight. Maybe they caught up with me, slipped me a pill and went through my work. Next they will want to resume their boring line of questioning: Why have you visited the Central Library (or archives or records department) and accessed information of so-and-so? Why do you type in the middle of the night? We have heard that you write in Pinyin and not in our beautiful Chinese characters, they will say with more hurt pride than anger, as they pretend that they've not been into my apartment just days before, rifling through my papers and drawers and finding nothing but poetry and scribblings about the city. I am not so stupid as to leave incriminating evidence that will get me disappeared or, worse still, reformed for treason.

After it was clear that someone had gone through my things I watched the housekeeper more carefully whenever she came to clean. I gave the old witch only enough to mislead. Still I had no choice but to leave the city with a small bag and a few books, on the evidence that they'd been in my place again.

The phone book on the bedside table of the hotel had never been opened before, and I flicked to M for Cousin's name. Despite its unusualness, I did not expect to find so few who shared it, and not one conceded that they'd known him. With my first plan laid waste, I readied myself for a day in the archives. Yet moments before I shut the door, I remembered Cousin's wife. There were many who shared her name and after spending a couple of hours on the hotel's computer, I traced a woman with the exact name, around the same age. Perhaps luck was on my side, because by the time I placed the fourteenth call, I recognized the voice at the other end.

It is Huang Zhao. Your husband's cousin.

Who?

Huang Zhao—your husband's cousin.

My husband died more than forty years ago.

Oh . . . oh, I am sorry to hear that. Very sorry, I said.

Thank you, she said, but spilled water is hard to recover. Do you plan to visit me?

Yes, Cousin, I do.

I have been expecting you for a very long time. Please come as soon as you can, she said, giving me the address.

I hastened to take a taxi to her home; in the afternoon traffic of a bustling city, it took almost two hours. The apartment block rose sixty floors into the air and its marbled floors, salmon-pink bricks, row of drivers in black sedans waiting outside to drive their *tai-tais* to appointments made me nervous. Why had she been waiting for me?

A string of women at the front desk pointed me to the correct set of elevators.

I was let in by a brisk housekeeper who took me into a gilded room to wait. From the vases filled with cream roses to the wallpaper, down to the rugs covering the floors, everything was threaded with gold.

An elderly woman, though not a frail one, walked into the room. I had to look carefully to be certain that this was the same person I had last seen more than forty years before, when as a student I had gone in search of a missing mother. The grey mouse had become a ginger cat, or maybe had been swallowed by one. Dressed in a matching cream-and-gold skirt and cardigan, she blended so seamlessly with the wallpaper that I feared if she stood before it, she'd vanish.

Her warm words threw me.

Young Zhao, I am happy to see you.

I had not been called Young Zhao for a very long time.

I apologize that I am late . . . the traffic, I said, pointing out of the high rise and towards the buildings, cranes, and the cars scattering like ants outside her window.

You are already decades late. What are a few more hours? She said, inviting me to sit.

You have been expecting me?

What took you so long?

Curiosity was great but not so much impetus. But then after all these years, something changed. I met someone to help my plans along . . .

Ah, she said, with an odd wink that startled me.

No . . . I began, but changed tack instead: I am sorry to hear of Cousin's death.

He gave me a son before he died, she said without a pause.

You have done well, I said, gesturing to the finery of the room.

My son is a prosperous businessman. Also his father's son, she said with an almost undetectable wince.

Then I congratulate you.

No need.

Cousin, I said, straightening in my chair as she fiddled with a large diamond stud in her ear. When I came to see you and Cousin many decades ago, you said that my mother had not been to visit you then. Do you remember that?

She nodded, then spoke, in a calm, cool voice.

I have much to tell you about that day and that time. I remember that afternoon when you came in search of your mother as if it were just yesterday. But now, well, I am getting old and I had started to fool myself that it had not happened; that none of it had. But finally, finally, you called. But Young Zhao, she said, leaning towards me, you must be ready to hear what I have to say because it will not be easy for you.

Yes, I nodded. My heart had been shattered long before and beneath my skin were only fragments. Words were like dust.

About three months before you arrived, she said, your mother had indeed come to see us. I was not honest with you then for reasons that I hope you might one day understand . . . those were such different times.

Yes.

Perhaps because we ate bitter then, we are here today . . . the Chairman knew we would have to endure terrible hardship to reach a new world.

She took a glass from the tray of tea and water that had been delivered to us.

I leant forward in my chair, trying to hasten her story.

Your mother, when she came to see us, well, I almost didn't recognize her. She looked older than her thirty years and she was weak . . .

Cousin stopped, took a sip of water from the delicate glass cupped in her hands.

By the time she reached the county seat she hadn't eaten for days, or had barely had much at all, Cousin said. Still, she'd made it from your village, a treacherous journey to be sure, so I knew she was still a defiant spirit. I was at home that day, while your cousin was at work.

I asked her why she'd come. I was alarmed: I knew that people had been instructed not to leave their villages no matter how bad their suffering. We were fighting for China's future, weren't we? Still, I had heard the stories of people starving across the county. Your mother said she had come to warn us, her cousin and me, about what was happening. That a terrible injustice was taking place in her village and that she needed my husband, her cousin, to alert the Party authorities in Beijing. I could see from her face that she had witnessed terrible things: the decomposing bodies of those who had died along the roads . . . from starvation and sometimes one heard people had been stopped in their tracks by the army, not that I ever saw that myself, no . . .

But Cousin . . .

No matter, Cousin said, silencing my question softly with her hand because we both knew that if I spoke now, a decades-long spell might be broken. Your mother came to ask her cousin to help her, to help your village, she continued. It was a terrible mistake. She didn't know him the way I did. He was not the boy she'd grown up with. The times, after all, demanded something from all of us and he had become a hardened man. I convinced her that if she pursued this with him, I would not be able to protect her. I fed your mother a bowl of congee. I found her a place where she would be safe with a friend I trusted; at least until we could think what to do.

Shall I go on? Cousin asked.

Yes, yes, I nodded.

Your mother remained hidden for two weeks. Each day, I took a ration of rice, some meat and vegetables to her and my friend; this would ensure your mother's agreement and silence from my friend, or so I thought. On the first day that I took her a meal, your mother ate as if she'd never seen food before. When the first pang was satiated she stopped suddenly, pushed the plate away and demanded to know why I had access to such food when the surrounding villages in our county were starving to death. That is how the world seems to work, isn't it, I said. Those that have must eat and those that do not . . . well. Your mother softened when she learned that I was three months pregnant.

Cousin's story was interrupted when, from the depths of the apartment, there came a sudden whoop, a child on the run. Within seconds there was pounding at the door, followed by a child and a woman in uniform.

I'm sorry, Tai Tai, said the woman to Cousin. He wanted to see who your visitor was.

No matter, no matter, said Cousin, taking the child, a little boy of about five years old with plump folded wrists and a thick padding of flesh that covered him from top to bottom.

Hush, hush, cooed Cousin. You see, I am talking to someone. I will take you for a walk as soon as I am done speaking to him. For now, go to your room, we are speaking about grown-up business.

Only after he was coaxed away with promises of sweets, television and toys, did the child reluctantly leave the room.

Cousin resumed, resetting her tone to melancholy: Because of the famine many, many women could not become pregnant, or if they did they lost their babies. I was lucky, wasn't I . . . she said and took another sip of water.

Some days I think my husband was a man who had a dream for a new China, but other days . . . other days, well, I think my husband became a man who loved his Party and his country too much. He did everything and anything to keep up appearances: even the meagre amounts of grain that should have gone to the people of our village were locked away before being sent elsewhere. She dabbed her entire face with a delicate white handkerchief that she removed, like a magician, from within her elegant folds. What I must tell you next . . . I thought I could keep your mother safe, and I did for almost two weeks. But we were betrayed. Then again, who knows, she said, looking out of the window as if a new thought had struck her . . . my friend had two small children and no husband, so perhaps the food I gave was not enough for what they needed. And I was so hungry all the time myself . . . My friend went to see my husband at his office one day. She told him everything and when he heard what had been happening and what had been kept from him, well, his first stop was to see me. He was not kind. He punished me and I understood that day that I was never to betray him. Your cousin's next step was to seek out your mother. I knew I had to get to her first . . . but it took me a long time to make it there. I was in pain. Terrible pain. Of course by the time I reached her, he had found her. I heard afterwards how she'd shamed him before many people for what was happening, starving his villagers, she said, while he ate like a lord. And then she pleaded—for your sake, her son's, she said—that China had to be saved from this famine, this torture. Unbowed, she told him, Cousin, you are not a hero but a traitor if you let us all die, not a saviour, but a coward.

He accused her of being an agent whose mind had been poisoned by rightists. But should I continue? Cousin asked as she fidgeted with her glass, her handkerchief, her diamond stud.

Go on, Cousin.

By the time I reached them, your mother was being paraded down the streets. I begged, pleaded with him to let her go, but what was I? A mouse that could be kicked away. I want you to know that I did not let her go alone for a minute of that ordeal,

Cousin said, wiping away tears. Every step she walked so did I, because her fate had become my own and that of my unborn child. Finally, she was taken into the village square where her life was taken from her. That was where I buried her later that night.

I cannot say what I felt as I sat perfectly still and watched Cousin crumble into herself, her face dissolving into the carpet. What was the strangeness I felt inside myself? Was it relief that I knew what had happened to my mother? Was it immeasurable sadness at how her life had ended? Was it grief and delayed mourning and anger and hurt and deep pride at what she had done? Was it finally knowing what I had already known for all those years? Was it the lengthening and stretching of the deep cracks within me?

Or was it filial love being awakened and reinforced and felt, as if anew?

Yes. Yes, it was.

29

THE AMERICAN HOUSE

Dear Friend,

They say this is the very last day of spring. I guess they must be right, because dusk settles slowly over Harlem, everyone ambles a bit more leisurely these days, strangers often pause beneath my window, perhaps to take in the softer air, before walking off, suddenly seized by some urgency elsewhere.

If I am not recovered, perhaps I can say that I am starting to live again. I took a short trip down South to visit a cousin, and it was here I learned that I had not been abandoned entirely. Some friends (at least) do not walk with eyes downcast into a room where I am standing, while others persist in their kindness, despite everything.

And man, each day my African anthology grows! I've received some one thousand pages already, including your wonderful piece. All these stories, poems, essays show your continent raising itself to full height. From Cape Town to Lagos, writers refuse silence. No, freedom is the prize and nothing less will do. Perhaps this old poet needs you more than you need him! The decade has not been without its challenges, and what relief, joy, to see the sun rising in the distance. If I am not reinvented, then at least I am reinvigorated for whatever must come.

I received your wire too. I don't know what to say. But I guess I had better find words: your refusal to judge, your understanding, does me much good. Your friendship means something solid in this world. Now, finally, what to say of your final paragraph? I have replayed it over and over again:

I will be in New York City, leaving in a few weeks, you wrote.

Did you try to tell me before? I guess you must have, but my silence did not encourage. By now, I think you must be packing your bags. Getting ready to leave your home for the many months away. Heading this way. To New York where I'm pleased you will take up a fellowship (I hope you have better luck at the college than I did—but then, times have changed). And then your final line: *I am coming, too, to see you.*

Until we are standing face to face after these many months and these many missives, how shall I pass the weeks, days, hours?

Perhaps I shall tell you more about the world that you asked about. Harlem. Where you said you hoped you'd find a place.

Will it meet your expectations? The heady days are long passed when we came here defiant, proud and buoyed by the times.

You asked some months ago, and I was too distracted to answer then: how did you come to find yourself in that fabled slip of time?

Because, they said in New York a Negro could live a little at least.

We packed light (dragging our baggage behind us) and in
Harlem we converged beneath the stars:

Musicians

    Playwrights

        Dancers

            Painters

                Novelists

                    Sculptors

                        Poets

                            Actors

                                Intellectuals

They called us the New Negro Movement or even the Negro
Literati (one of our number rechristened us the Niggerati; we
liked it more). How did it all happen, you wanted to know?

Man, someone sat down at a piano and caressed the keys in a
way that no one had done, so we said it was Harlem Stride.
Someone wrote a verse to a beat and we said, why, that's Jazz
Poetry. Skirts got shorter by the minute, waistlines dropped
lower, leg pants got wider and coats longer. Women danced with
women and called themselves sir (if they liked). Boys strolled out
of the shadows and to the front of the bar so they could dance
the cabaret. Did they call us queer? Black as the night? Well, we
didn't care! We were beautiful, fierce and smart as anything.
Language in a spectrum never before heard drifted down the
sidewalk and you had to be careful how you stepped. The blues
could not be escaped. (Anyway, who'd want to?) We rebelled and
produced, then slunk into clubs and corners to lick our wounds,
always taking our humanity by the handful.

But no.

No, friend.

That's what I'm meant to tell you.

Truth is, Harlem was the only place to go if you were poor. Black. Where you went if you were angry as hell and ready to speak freely. Where we could be ourselves. We were tired of being sad, so we added a carefree beat to the blues and made jazz. Writing, that respectable profession that sought to make a Negro a decent subject, became about tellin' tales. Heck, I didn't want to write about the upright! I wrote about the people who worked all day and night for a corner just to breathe.

And the parties! The Cotton Club on 142nd and Lenox was not for us regular folk. Not for any of us, with its black stages and white audiences and its Jim Crow. People came from the other side of the city in their thousands to Harlem for the spectacle of black folk dancing and singing. Where did Harlem party? In unmarked clubs and apartments that crowded up come Friday night and we, Harlem, after a fourteen-hour shift, dragged ourselves to these dances to spirit away the ache in our shoes. Let me mention too the:

Shoeshine boys

Bus boys

Waiters

Porters

Hairdressers

Tinkers

Tailors

Soldiers

Sailors

The unheralded were here, too. The unlovely and the tired. As we always are. I wrote for us.

How had I landed in the middle of it all? By the time Harlem found me, or I had found it, I had dropped out of university (the same one you're bound for), travelled to Africa as a mess boy on a boat, been a farm hand, a bus boy and a waiter! I was not, had never been, one thing or the other. (Is anyone ever?) Yet even the safe knowledge that I was a black man came into question. After one of those long boat journeys where I left American ports to awaken at strange new shores, I landed in the Belgian Congo and greeted my people like the long-lost brothers and sisters they were (as they remain). They said, "But you are a white man!" I started to argue, to ache, to argue some more, but what was the use? My Indian grandmother, my white slave-owning ancestry, had mixed my blood.

No matter, for I knew where my soul resided.

Back in the USA, was it fortuitous that the famous poet walked into the hotel in which I worked? Beside his napkin, knife and fork, I laid my scribblings. To my wonder (and relief) he called me a lyricist. Perhaps it was luck. Or hell, maybe it *was* the stars. Or we were just fed up all at the same time. No longer ashamed. No longer one thing or the other. Ready to open the doors and windows after such a long seclusion. Exclusion.

And then, in Harlem I found myself.

Could I be all of me, you ask? Sometimes, sure.

Did I fall in love? Sure. Didn't everyone?

Where? In the places where I could.

But I warn you that these Harlem streets can be rough, too.

I'd only been back a couple of days from my trip down South when, as I stood outside a hotdog stand on the sidewalk, a young pickpocket snuck up between me and an old man and lifted the wallet clear out of his pocket. He winked and tipped his hat before making off. These streets can be mean, crowded, loud, hot, and hellish, but it does me good to be back home.

The old Harlem though is gone. The writers and poets have fled these sidewalks for more urbane places (Paris and the likes).

I am still here. The words still linger, always will, while the melodies drift across space and time. These days the young no longer walk a Harlem stride. They write with a taste for assimilation, speaking of the I (but not we), their eyes to Europe. They pass me by and do not bother to wave as they go.

Am I still the Poet Laureate? Was I ever? I think my fall is complete, for I hear their chatter. The young ones call me out of touch behind my back; say my politics and racial pride belong to another era. Maybe they have a point. They have their new darlings. I am still broke, still hustling. They scoff when I enter a room, and ask not to be compared to me.

Fine. That's just fine. I can fall but I do not break.

I imagine you will say, Really, Langston—fall from grace? Certainly you may be out of favour, but isn't that too dramatic?

Only time can tell how I will be remembered.

Apostate?

Liar?

Pragmatist?

Poet?

Dreamer?

Send me a letter from the future, will you?

There. It has gone silent for just a moment (Harlem is never truly quiet). I wonder where you are. If you have boarded your boat yet. What you will do on that long journey. For now, I will get some sleep, although I do not imagine you will be out of mind. Soon.

Your Friend,
Langston

30

THE SHANGHAI BOOK CLUB

The days and weeks exhaled, a restiveness exacerbated by heat and panic so there was no space for living. Between night and dawn, when the city doesn't dare shut its eyes, neon signs from the Bund, the glinting of river boats, the endless hammering and shifting of construction materials conspired, while the need for vigilance kept me in its grip.

The finer details of my life had begun to come into focus. All of it: Andrew, my guilt about working for the government, and of course Kay, who had never been entirely out of my thoughts. A strange idea came to me in the blue light, Kamal asleep beside me: I had only recently stopped thinking of Kay's absence with grief, when really she had lived an exemplary, courageous life— the kind upon which freedom rests.

For myself, it was a revelation that a human life could have another reality dormant inside of it, or perhaps an entire soul, living, breathing just beneath the first (or is it the second; the real self?). So each day, while routine functions are performed—work, eating, sex—there is a truth undisclosed. Then one day, circumstances shift and only then, slowly—never suddenly—the narrative, the story, the person, is flipped and the other being rises to take the place of the first (or is it second?). And so here I was, attending my own life. Finally grieving fully for Kay, Andrew, and Zhao, too, and even for a younger self.

Soon after our confrontation, Arabile, too, disappeared. His secretary said he was working from home; that he had an unspecified infection and couldn't come to the office. I offered to deliver work to him, but was told that anything requiring his signature was to be couriered only. I didn't see or hear from Shan at all; her emails went unanswered and her phone was permanently off.

When Arabile reappeared after a week, he slunk past me at reception, barely greeted me, and shut the door to his office.

I walked in behind him.

"Are you all right?"

"Yep."

"Shan?"

He wrote something on a note pad, calmly and deliberately, sliding it across the table towards me.

You got her detained.

I stared at the piece of paper for a long while, before I scribbled back:

Where is she now?

Home again.

May I see her? I asked.

He tore the note carefully, diligently, into such small pieces that it gave the sense of a man who had lost his mind. Maybe he had.

Later that evening, just before six, someone came to my door as Zhao had first done, unbidden with the setting sun. Hearing the rap, I hoped it might be him. Come home so soon, I imagined I'd say, pretending that I'd not missed him or even noticed he'd been gone.

But it was Shan standing small and delicate in the passageway, younger than I'd ever seen her in jeans and a hoodie, a scarf pulled up to her chin.

"Come in?"

No, she shook her head, and motioned, so I grabbed my shoes where they stood at the door, and followed her outside.

"You OK?" she asked as we made our way out of the building and into the gardens.

"Are *you* all right?"

"I'm fine," she said, fixing her eyes on the ground.

"Arabile said you were . . ." I began, but she squeezed my arm hard, and jolted by the shot of pain, the act itself, I stopped.

It had just gone dark, the sky threaded with lavender and gold on what had been a remarkably clear day. Children ran between us in the maze and young and old lovers milled about the gardens laughing and speaking sweetly.

"I was asked some important life questions recently," Shan said.

"Yes?"

"I was asked about my practice, my friends, Arabile. My work with women. Some associations that I have made that were not good for me. And I have come to tell you, Beth, after much thought that it would be best . . . in the best interests of China

261

and Africa's relations . . . for your own country and your future . . ." she said, and I stood still to listen to the stoic tone in her voice, ". . . whatever you were working on that was ill-considered, you should give it up. China is a great country and we are happy to be here, so must do the right thing."

"Yes," I said.

"I came to say you need to look after yourself." Shan squeezed my arm again, softer this time, pulled me sharply towards her and turned into the maze. In her palm I could just about see the message that she must've typed earlier on her phone. *Passport taken. Will try to leave via Hong Kong. Dad will help.*

She quickly deleted the message as she returned the phone to her pocket.

"I just came to wish you luck and say you need to make good plans. For your life. Better decisions for yourself."

"Of course," I said. "If I did anything ill-considered, then that was a mistake," I said, replicating her leaden sentences and speaking for the benefit of the seen as much as the unseen. "I will not do anything to harm my country; or China. No, after all, I love your country as I do my own," I said, and knew it to be sincere.

Shan faced me.

"You will do as agreed?"

Yes, I nodded but remained silent: I'd emailed the manuscripts to someone, so I hoped they existed out of the country now; that Andrew had received everything and managed to print it.

Shan wiped tears away with the back of her sleeve. Even though she seemed fragile I knew that she wasn't. For a crazy moment I imagined I was standing with neither Shan nor Kay, but with essence, a rebellious being, a warrior spirit, confined not to body, shape or time, always drifting without settling.

But of course this was Shan. She took my hand in hers, met my eyes briefly and walked away.

31

CAPE'S CONFESSION

It is the last day that I'll meet my commissioner like this.

Soon he will move to the next file in his batch of cases that he carries in a scuffed leather satchel. Other families who require his succour and kindness more will receive his benediction. Perhaps the woman I saw in the foyer that morning wrapped in a dull head scarf and blanket thrown over the triangle of her body, her face a shadow of a greater grief that has already passed, will finally hear what happened to her husband/daughter/son; will find a body, or at least understand who was responsible for the death/disappearance/maiming. Perhaps my commissioner cleanses his soul with a course of Hail Marys or Our Fathers, kneeling in the privacy of his chambers, or his home, or wherever he finds himself given his direct line to God. But prayer is no longer open to me. My confession is my plea for forgiveness. But will it set me free?

Good morning. Today, please finish your story, he says with a note of sternness. I've drawn out the good will of the commission, lengthening my tale, stretching my testimony to fit my ambitions.

Last time we spoke, you indicated that it was your belief that Samuel Nathaniel Jacobs, his finger hovers over my file . . . or

Sammy Jacobs, had given over incriminating information, obtained from the victim herself in the form of a diary, to the security branch. And that these were the circumstances which led Kalliope, Kay, he says, softening his tone, to her ultimate terrible death.

Yes.

During our line of enquiry, he says, it has come to our attention that Sammy Jacobs, I am afraid to say, passed on some years back.

Yes, I nod, I know this. Was that not why I was here, after all: to confess to his death?

My commissioner continues, Let me specify that you are saying you didn't betray your friend, have maintained that all along, despite the fact that such a claim was made in a police report, drafted in ... There is a tone of finality about his sentences, clipped and contained now.

I am not yet done, though, I interrupt and an audible tittering rises from the Peanut Gallery and press.

He sighs loudly, so I imagine his lament is searching for God above the ceiling, above the clouds.

May I continue with my testimony? I say.

All right ... yes, but we must finish today.

Yes, I say. It was only some years after Kay's death that I finally understood fully how Kay had been betrayed.

Ma Mouth-Breather is there, I sense her, even though she is perfectly still. My parents are in their usual place, quietly sober and remorseful for having neglected their parental and civic duties—they will tell me this for the rest of their lives—and of

266

course, of course I will forgive them for being the sort of cold, uncommunicative parents who shouldn't have had children. Lucie, Kay's mother, is seated in the third row; she rests her chin on her balled-up fists as she rocks back and forth, back and forth.

After leaving high school, I applied and was accepted to university on a full bursary; the new South Africa wanted its future educated and qualified. It was during my second year as I sat on the main campus steps one afternoon—with a clear view of anyone passing—that I saw a familiar face. It took me moments to place him. I erased the sideburns that grazed his cheeks, the tuft of hair from his chin. Karl. It was Karl.

Karl? My commissioner says.

Yes, Kay's friend, Karl, who you'll recall had refused military service, had taken her under his wing.

He was a memory. A memory coupled to devastation. I don't know . . . maybe that explains why I rose and walked behind him. One block, two, until suddenly he turned left and entered a building. I trailed him to a small office, watched as he fished keys from the pocket of his jeans, fiddled with the door and let himself in. For a long time, I stood outside his office, uncertain why I'd followed him.

He was a lecturer teaching political science, and I began to attend his classes every week, sitting always at the back. I thought he saw me once, that he must have recognized me, because his eyes stayed on me for some time.

One such day, during a debate about South Africa during the eighties, a question arose about collaboration. I saw some traces of the person I'd once known: Karl carefully reasoned with his

267

students, agreeing with some sentiments, gently disagreeing with others, when a student sitting in the front raised his hand.

But collaboration was a choice! A wilful choice to betray someone in the interests of self-preservation, right? Shit, man . . . sorry . . . I mean to say . . . it's not like I'm judging, just talking facts here: many in history have been tortured . . . but what makes one man sing and another . . . yes, or woman (he said to a chorus of voices from behind) remain resolute? Either self-preservation kicks in, or sacrifice. Some have the ability to martyr themselves for the greater cause, while others, most, just don't. Simple as that, man.

All the while I watched Karl's face remain unmoved as he calmly explained that it was more complex than that; that many other factors needed to be taken into account.

When the lecture was over, I walked to his podium and waited to be noticed.

"Hi—you need to ask me anything?" he said.

"You don't remember me?"

"Should I?" he said over his shoulder, as he started to pack up his notes.

"I was Kay's friend." I had not said her name out loud in years, and the ease with which I said it brought an ache and a release.

He turned, to stare at me.

"How did you betray her?" I asked. Was it the fact that he'd discussed with his students a matter that had been so close to him from a remove, with cool precision? Then again, I had often thought it strange that Karl claimed to know nothing. Kay had trusted him; more, I thought they must have been lovers.

Why did you think this? asks my commissioner now, just going through the motions, aware that he is only an actor in my script.

The older I became, the more I could see and understand matters which had been right before me at the time, but which I couldn't comprehend then.

"Let us talk, but not now," he said, writing down his number on a scrap of paper as a student came to speak to him.

I waited for her to leave.

"Please," he said.

"I should have spoken to you properly about Kay, her death, years ago. I can wait five more minutes."

"I don't know what you think you know. Or what gives you the right?"

"Tell me then."

I walked beside him to his office.

Only once we were seated, when it was clear I would go nowhere, did he tell me what I'd come to hear.

Please would you tell us? My commissioner asks, as the room tilts, their ears and hearts set.

He told me this: he had been arrested months before Kay's death. I pause for a long while until there is utter silence in the hall, only the soft whirr of electronic equipment and the click of cameras can be heard.

Karl told me he had tried to protect Kay at first. But he had been tortured, threatened, his future lay in shreds, he said. Finally he relented and betrayed Kay. He was instructed to pass information, false information, to her and to introduce her to a policeman, who was working under the guise of being a comrade.

He didn't think that they . . . that anyone . . . would actually murder her. Just scare . . . intimidate her. But the agent was most likely the person who placed a defective bomb in her hands.

And Sammy?

Who? said Karl.

Sammy. Sammy who led the police to you? I asked. I had believed Sammy to be the informant. It seemed so obvious, didn't it? Sammy, the skollie, the loser. He must have led the police to you?

I don't know who that is, Karl insisted, and anyway there were plenty who might have given my name to the security police.

I'm lost, my commissioner says. Karl just told you all of this?

Karl said that if I ever told anyone he would deny all of it, turning the tables and accusing me instead. It would be his word against mine, "a respected academic versus you—a young girl, desperate to dream up a reason to escape your guilty conscience," he'd said. I'm sure he, along with whoever planned Kay's murder, are the people who are making this claim against me. But then, of course, he was also right. I had a guilty conscience. I was guilty.

Explain . . . please, my commissioner says.

Don't you see? After what Sammy had done to me, I spread the word that he'd been responsible for Kay's death. I told someone . . . maybe in confidence at first, without thinking it would harm him . . . but then it became an active idea that he should be blamed; that it *was* him and that I had no business, no desire to shield him. That it had to have been him who betrayed Kay. Back then, to be an informer, an impimpi, was a worse sin than being a gangster and certainly worse than being a rapist. I spoke the words and it became a fact. A set of insinuations that caught fire, so Sammy became an outcast among outcasts. A liar among liars. He became no one. I found out that his family had received a pension payout years after Sammy's father's death . . . which explained the newly bought items. I also learned that after years of depression and drugs, Sammy had left a note saying very little: yes, that he'd done some terrible things but that he'd not betrayed Kay, his childhood friend. Finally, after what Karl said, I believed him. Up until that moment with Karl, I had thought I'd wanted Sammy dead. Yet his death, my revenge, tasted bitter.

You were a child . . . and he was not innocent of inflicting harm.

Yes. I would never have forgiven him for raping me. I wanted him to pay. Still, I had my life to recover, but wasn't he, as Kay had always said, a product of his environment? What the system had designed? A victim of his own circumstances, as much as a perpetrator? I took away any chance Sammy might have had for redemption.

Yes, my commissioner says, even though he seems to doubt me now, yes, he says. We have come to the end of this session and case. Any further investigations will be taken up . . .

Won't he be called? Karl? Held to account? I say.

That will be determined by someone else.

Won't he stand trial? Or at least be questioned, so he can tell us who the operative was that placed the bomb in her hands? Perhaps it was Karl himself? These things need to be determined, settled, I say.

This is not that sort of hearing. Those are not my decisions because this is not a court of law, he says, but a place of healing and forgiveness.

But I don't want to simply forgive. I do not want those who've hidden in the shadows of Kay's death to vanish without a confession, I say, allowing my voice to rise to the furthest reaches of the room—a moment of bravery, truth, clarity that may never come again and so I savour it. There is a sudden barrage of pictures from the press.

Wasn't Karl, too, a product of his environment? Just like Kay, Sammy, me? Wasn't he too damaged and broken by the same system in equal and opposite ways? Child soldiers all of us. Yet the war was waged against and within us too. Karl must speak!

My commissioner looks at me with an expression that I interpret to be pity, so I straighten my back and look away.

You have come here and spoken for days, made us understand how much this young person's life was valued; how special she was. How cherished. What an abomination Kay's death was. Her mother knows what she did not know before. You, too, have confessed, he says. And you have voiced how you were harmed. I believe you. But you must forgive yourself. Thank you, he says, ending the day's session.

Of course there would be no trial. Still, I had come to give life back to Kay. To shed the accusations and the guilt I'd lived with like a second skin. But in wanting to free myself, I'd had to place blame on him, on Karl, before the cameras, before my Peanut Gallery. No, I didn't want him to continue to live silently with the sin of his guilt. Guilt is no confession.

272

When I walk from the hall, I am aware of the eyes that trail me: there is Ma Mouth-Breather, loyal to the end, my parents in perpetual shame; Lucie, who wipes her eyes and tries to smile as I go by, but does not manage. I pass a row of chairs, and find a delegation of comrades seated close to the back. Have they attended each day? If so, I'd not seen them before. They stand and shake my hand vigorously.

"We knew you were innocent! We hear you got into the presidency, even without our help? Still, now we know where you are, we will be there for you," they say through pained smiles. As I reach the last row, I see him, Karl, seated in a distant corner, his eyes reddened, his face a mask as he tries to hide behind the day's paper, rolled into a canister in his hand. Perhaps I'm mistaken, because I can barely see my feet before me. Before I exit the room entirely, I turn to look at Lucie and I am grateful when she lifts her hand to wave, or to wish me well, or perhaps even to offer me their, her and Kay's, wish for the great post-apartheid dream: a normal life.

32

BENEATH YELLOW MOUNTAIN

But this mountain will not leave me alone, wanting not only sweet soft words but everything I have left, which is not so much really.

Fine: you are the pearl of perfection. It is the thread of dawn that falls from your brow sewing us back together again. Is that enough? More terrible poetry? Whatever, like the Western children say in the city and now our children too.

~

I made my way from the old county seat, and did not really know where I would go next. It is strange but when a question is answered after forty years, it's not fulfilment but emptiness that remains.

I let my legs walk me to the station, and there I thought of returning at least to see if you were all right. Really, I do not know what effect my words will have on you, or how you will make any sense of them, I only know that you will.

At first Old Lin's sister just stared at me when I arrived in the middle of the night knocking softly at her door. She stepped aside and let me in, never asking why I had come, because of course she already knew. It was not so much that the mountain called, but that she had offered me an impossible deal, imprisoning me with her words. Perhaps I came to see if she had been set free. I saw that she had not, that her plan had backfired and now here we both were, trapped. She brought me a bowl of hot soup, placed it on the table before she rested her head on my back and wept.

The next morning she said to me, Did you find your mother?

Yes, I said. I took a bunch of the yellowest flowers found at the city's market. Tulips, can you imagine, I said, yellow tulips in this cold, from Holland, well, actually, the flower seller said they were from Kenya, but tulips! I laid it before the town square, which still stands, and I recited a poem by Du Fu, right there, so the people stepped around the madman reading poetry early in the day.

She smiled and went to cook breakfast.

In the evenings, I unroll a thin foam mattress in a room that is almost empty aside from a chair and a desk and there I sleep on the wooden floor. The window, if the weather permits, is always slightly ajar, so the mountain air fills my head and pushes me to safe dreams.

But, is it strange to you that I have come here? Unguarded and broken? Do you worry about my sanity? Me, too, but somehow, here, the condemned and cursed must find a way to peace, here in nature's palm, where we are so little, so insignificant, we can maybe think a new way is possible. See how much hope this life has too? Each time I am low I see the face of the young girl from the square on that terrible day and somehow I know I must rise. Find courage. Or do you think me crazy? Probably I am.

I do not know when I will leave here. Perhaps it is the mountain that keeps me, or maybe it is the strange alchemy of Feng's memories, but here I stay. Some days we speak about the past. Some days we say nothing at all to each other, only stare at the mountain. It is that kind of mountain. But then, what else? And so here I remain, somehow, still living and finding my way to hope.

Will I see you again, my friend? Perhaps you are angry because I have burdened you with my story, and so anyway you do not want to see me.

But no, I don't think so.

Finally, after a thousand confessions, one more.

Before I knocked at your door that evening searching for a word, I had already seen you from my window (it has a nicer view than yours). You were walking between the thick folds of the maze thinking you were alone, but I stood at my window and watched you. Something you did, I don't know what it was, but something reminded me of my mother: the way you moved or plucked a dead leaf from a branch, how defiant you seemed. I knew before you did that you would carry my burden. I knew too, before we ever spoke, that I would trust you and that you would not let me down.

Perhaps I will come to find you one day. You know, I have never left China? For now, though, I am here beneath my mountain. I cannot say for how much longer.

But here I remain.

Your Friend
Zhao

33

THE AMERICAN HOUSE

Dear Friend,

I saw you seated on a wooden chair outside a café on the corner of Fifth and 42nd the other day: the steam from your coffee catching the morning air, drifting towards me, its ethereal fingers stopping short. Your legs were folded grandly beneath the table, and I was surprised that you were taller than I had imagined; the curl of your hair swept down across your forehead every few seconds, so you had to push it back, and the more time wore on, the more agitated you became until you exhaled and pushed back your hair entirely. The manuscript that you looked up from every few seconds (were you looking to see from which direction I might arrive?)—tell me, what was that? Perhaps a book of short stories? Or perhaps that novel that you've been threatening to start, but which is always a moment away. You said you might use the name District Six in the title. Fine decision.

Seeing you seated there, here, in my city, real and quite lovely, stopped me in my tracks, so my feet became solid earth. You were not a figment of my imagination after all.

You did not see me, for I remained there on the corner, immovable. To my shame, I had to be asked after twenty minutes to stop loitering and so I bid you farewell and walked back home, never once turning back.

Why, you will ask, did you not come and sit with me as we had arranged? Why did you not at least order a coffee, leaving it there to grow cold and bitter, and then we might finally have taken the measure of each other off the page as we had agreed to do?

I cannot say why I did not have the nerve. Perhaps . . . perhaps, it has been the steady unveiling of myself to you that gave me pause. Even though I hope you will know that I am, have always been, true to what mattered most, you will know too that I've made choices which almost saw me come undone. Yet, still now I do not think there was another way. Did I fear your opinion so much that it made me turn and keep walking? I guess so.

I suppose, too, there was the idea that you might slide your hand across the table, and with your devil-may-care attitude, with your eyes boring into me, you might expect . . . what? I would have seen your intention, as you would have seen mine. But the world is not blind and it waits for a man like me to trip. It always does.

And then? And then, I do not know.

Perhaps there was another notion still: that all this time I had been duping myself and all you wanted was to show me gratitude for getting your work published in an international anthology; to say thank you for the friendship and guidance. Am I an old fool then, who dreams of long languid days in the company of one still unblemished by life (by this writing life)?

Is it comfort or torment to know that you walk in the same world as me? Not across the oceans or in another city, but that you are here in my town, safe and glorious. But so it must remain. What then have we left to say to one another?

Goodbye, Friend. Goodbye.

Ever yours, Langston

34

THE SHANGHAI BOOK CLUB

The interrogation rooms of Pudong International Airport were on a windowless subterranean floor. The metal chairs and tables were bent and bruised in all the right places. The angle-poised khaki lamps and two-way mirrors seemed reproduced from a defunct Cold War manual.

The officer rolled up her shirtsleeves punctiliously: first left, then right, searching for a natural crease, folding each to the apex of her elbow. She took a full five minutes, I noticed from the clock demolishing seconds like a sledgehammer behind her head.

"I have all day," she said in polished clipped sentences, leaning back and tapping pearly pink nails against the table. The reality of what was happening sat heavy in the room in the space between our eyes like a fight film on silent.

"You know that my flight leaves in three hours, so perhaps you could just tell me what it is that I am supposed to be carrying that is illicit. And who on earth would say that I posed a security risk of any sort? Better yet, call my consulate. Whatever you seem to think you have the right to do, you do not. I am a diplomat; protocol as well as several conventions insist that I may be neither searched nor detained." I was bluffing, of course. The way I'd left, she couldn't call.

"Yes, you said that already. But we are not doing anything illegal. How can it be illegal to check your luggage after a call, a threat, has been reported? And as you said, it is protocol, not law, that says we should not search your bags. We would be remiss if we did not investigate. But you should know that we informed your embassy that we would be speaking to you."

"You called the embassy?"

"Yes."

Knockout.

Two days after Shan's visit, Arabile sent me a message at the office to say he'd be away for a week; the note was incomprehensibly vague, yet I understood they would be leaving the country. I felt no small degree of guilt for my part in this and the fact that Shan's aging parents would be denied their daughter.

I had already started to consider how I'd leave Shanghai but it turned out there was no need. The ambassador in Beijing, a man I'd known for two decades, called me one afternoon.

"Elizabeth . . . Beth," he said in his bassoon's voice. "You have been very busy."

"Excuse me, sir?" I said, "What do you mean?" He never called and I knew him to be a man who went leisurely to lunch despite the backlog of paperwork that would never be completed.

"Man . . . you know what I mean. But we cannot speak too much now . . . I have a flight leaving in a few hours. I wanted to be the one to tell you, to give you the news personally, that we have decided that you should be redeployed."

"What? Why?"

"We will speak when we are back in South Africa about the why and wherefores," he said.

"At least tell me where," I said, too stunned to pretend.

"We will have to speak about it. I don't know yet what Pretoria wants to do with you."

"You won't tell me why or where, John, yet you say you're redeploying me? What's going on?" I wasn't innocent but I hadn't imagined that I would lose my job over what had so far amounted to an idea, an unfulfilled plan, a threat of a manuscript which might no longer exist if it had been apprehended before it reached Andrew.

"Eish, Lizzie come now. How long have we two known each other? Ten years? Fifteen?"

"Twenty," I said.

"Twenty years. So let us not play these games. No no no, Elizabeth. We will speak. Take a few weeks off, visit Cape Town, swim in the ocean, cook your mother some nice stews."

"My parents have passed."

"Oh. My condolences! Anyway. When you've done vacationing, we will speak about things."

"What are the reasons, John?"

"You are well acquainted with the Foreign Service Bill; I know how detailed you've always been. Paragraph 5.2."

I was being recalled for misconduct, still under investigation.

"But come now, Beth. We will talk another time. Not over the phone like this."

"When do you want me gone?"

"Today," he said, and made a series of excuses about not miss-ing his flight, and was gone.

Most of the consular staff were at lunch when the ambassador called, so I packed a few things, drafted an email to them explain-ing what I could, and left before any of them returned. I'd fallen on my sword and it felt blunter and rustier than I could have known.

I went home to pack my bags and book a ticket. The typewriter Zhao had given me was the only worldly possession that I chose to save, and I sent this ahead to South Africa, carefully wrapped in a box stuffed with Styrofoam chips, marked "very fragile." It was a folly that cost me two weeks' salary, but was made up for by the fact that I'd have to leave my books behind. I didn't think my consulate would care to forward them.

I'd not seen Kamal for days. Our nights together had been teetering to an end, the sex becoming less curious and more routine. Anyway, we'd always understood that it was friendship for which we were destined. I'd call him when I could.

I took only two bags.

~

After the hours of interrogation and a missed flight, the officer took her time filling out a series of forms.

What I feared was that something more incriminating than a manuscript might be discovered in my luggage. Say a small parcel of some illegal substance or other, planted moments before by another official. My embassy must have been aware of my association with a suspected dissident, if not of our amateur attempt at a collaborative manuscript, to the vexation of the Chinese government. If I got out of this mess, what beyond? When I returned home, was it only dismissal that awaited me, or a public shaming? Claims of my having done far worse whispered into a reporter's ear, and if nothing could be found to substantiate them, no matter, my reputation would lie in ruins anyway. For everything I'd just given up and was about to, I still didn't know whether Andrew had in fact printed the papers or if our accounts had been hacked, the files apprehended somewhere in cyber-space and bleached of everything.

All the while the officer and I performed our routine.

Only when she came to the last page, each requiring our signatures, did she speak again:

"You are almost free to go. Please sign here, and here. Perhaps you will come back to China one day," she said.

"So you found nothing, as I said?"

"If you do visit China again, you will be more careful," she said, talking over me.

"I work here. I will be back in a few days," I said; despite my bluff having been called, I resisted giving her the satisfaction of showing I knew I was beat.

"Of course," she said, smiling at me. "Surely you would not leave your books, so carefully arranged, behind."

"What?"

"What?" she echoed.

"How do you know about my bookshelf?" I said. "My books . . ."

"I don't know what you mean," she said, and stamped the forms hard.

How long had they (she?) been aware of me, my life, and the odd yet intimate detail of my bookshelf? I reasoned that I'd been watched for some time, perhaps as early as a year ago when I'd first met Zhao. I couldn't know for certain, but Ayi must have been complicit, allowing them into my home when I was at work, maybe riffling through my things herself and reporting back to them. Despite my anguish at such an intimate betrayal, I knew she wouldn't have had a choice.

I spent the rest of the evening in a neglected airport lounge, my access to the usual one strangely rescinded, and I had to scour the airport for another for the night.

By now my colleagues would have known about my dishonourable recall, because no one called or bothered to check on me, allowing me to slink out of the country. I tried calling Kamal from the airport, but he didn't answer, and as my last act on Chinese soil I sent Andrew one line saying I'd arrive the next day, hoping he would still be willing to drop everything on a last-minute call from me. Boarding the plane early the next morning, I turned on reaching the top of the ramp, so my eyes might locate something familiar in the city I'd lived in for more than a year. But what could I see through the fog falling over it, stubbornly refusing to give me even one last goodbye?

~

Here.

She would stay for a while, Beth decided as she watched for

the train that passed every thirty minutes, sending the place into convulsions so cups had to be taken off pegs where they were drying, to be buried in cupboards, while windows and floorboards reverberated rhythmically. Her eyes hooked onto the line of surfers bobbing in the Atlantic Ocean. The blue filled her view from corner to corner.

Tearing off a loose needle of wood, she noticed the window-frame was rotting and would have to be replaced.

Beth had found the one-bedroom flat beyond the row of trendy coffee shops, down a forgotten alley still undiscovered by the real estate agents who were renewing and remaking everything, evicting hapless tenants without a second glance. With the pension money that she'd accumulated and a small inheritance left by her parents, Beth had made an offer in an afternoon, moving in within the month.

The flat was sparsely furnished. She liked the cleanness of it all. A fresh start.

The brown leather couch that had been the first piece of furniture Beth had bought stood across from the window, so she didn't have to rise to watch waves crashing into an iridescent shoreline. She didn't need to rearrange herself to breathe in the sweet salty sea air that entered the place persistently, browning the walls and leaving crystal flecks on the windows.

A newly purchased metal-and-wood bookshelf stood against the opposite wall, almost empty aside from a few items, one being Kamal's newest book, *The Burglars*. It didn't mention, thank or acknowledge the wife and child in London to whom he'd returned. Certainly not Beth.

The other books: Richard Rive's *Buckingham Palace, District Six*, *Not Without Laughter* by Langston Hughes, and a bound copy of a book of letters Hughes had written to South African writers, including Rive. The owner of the crammed store where she'd found the books had insisted she take all the books for the price of two. She accepted the gift and made a mental note to shop there again. And when, days later, Beth heard a developer was trying to get the bookstore demolished to make way for a luxury high-rise, she signed up with a group planning to protest the area's hasty redevelopment.

On a lower level of the bookshelf were Zhao's writings. Andrew had given them to Beth on the day that he'd collected her from the airport. They were bound now into a thick manuscript. She and Andrew had hardly spoken then, the ache at seeing each after all those months unexpected and real. When they'd arrived at the hotel, he'd passed her the final papers—respecting her wishes, he'd said—dissolving their union. Silently she'd gotten out of the car.

Since her return home—first to Johannesburg before Cape Town—Beth found that she couldn't arrange a meeting with anyone in consular services, even with colleagues she'd known for decades. The ones who remained in government to fight its decimation saw her departure as a betrayal. And the dirty ones—who owned weekend houses in sleepy fishing villages or wore Swiss watches as a not-so-secret sign that there was a corresponding Swiss bank account—wouldn't take her calls or acknowledge her emails. She was being permitted an exit without further scandal. All she had to show for the career for which she had given up

Andrew and perhaps half of her life was a modest pension and a degree of infamy.

Still, it was time to start anew, and before moving to Cape Town, Beth called Andrew to make peace, to say cursorily but earnestly that she'd forgiven him. To apologize for their Shanghai conversation.

Also, Andrew . . . you were right. I let the people down. I let you down.

And I let you down, too. It's never too late, you know, Beth. It never is.

Yes.

Friendship? Andrew had suggested. Perhaps. He wasn't seeing *her* . . . or anyone, he'd added.

We've just gotten divorced, she laughed. We can meet for coffee when you're in Cape Town, Beth said before asking him for the couch. Then with her worldly possessions she moved back to Cape Town—home—maybe to start again, or at least to gather up the parts of herself that had fallen along the way.

Zhao's old typewriter stood on a mosaic side table just off the kitchen. Beth had wound a yellowing sheet of paper, found in a forgotten drawer, into the old machine.

She picked up Zhao's manuscript and folded herself into the couch. If she were to find a publisher, under whose name could she do it? Zhao, already on the run from Chinese authorities months earlier, would be further exposed and endangered.

Shan had proposed a solution during one of their regular conversations. Settled in San Francisco with Arabile, Shan had offered to try to get the manuscript published on her end. Shan wasn't angry after all that had happened, and remained adamant that their project must be seen through. When Arabile had stepped into the frame one afternoon, Beth had waved cheerily, hopeful that he'd got over what had happened, but either he didn't see her, or so he pretended.

"You think the Chinese authorities would ignore it if it were published, Shan?"

"Only care what is said about China inside of China," she said between mouthfuls of something that Arabile had just cooked and which looked delicious. "What you publish in South Africa about China doesn't really count, Beth!"

"Well, it will matter to my government. But fine, say I go ahead and find a willing publisher, under whose name?"

"Pseudonym."

"That would make it feel almost fictional."

"You could do that."

"What?"

"Fiction." — T R U T H

"No . . ."

"Why not? You write."

"Not really. For work only these days."

". . . That's enough. Anyway, what else? You can't do it under my name, Arabile would never forgive you," she said mischievously, loudly, with a wink as she sipped tea from a huge mug. "Anyway, when everything settles, my parents will visit and you know my name is famous."

"Do you think I'll hear from him again?"

"Yes," said Shan, her eyes filling with tears. She said she cried all the time now that she was pregnant. Even during commercials.

"How would he even locate me?"

"He did before, no?"

"I suppose."

"Anyway. I must go. Think about it."

"I have to go, too . . ."

"You have a date with someone nice?"

"I'm going to visit my parents' graves. Clean up . . . it's been years," Beth said, rearranging the posy of dahlias that she'd got for this purpose.

"Hey, take care of yourself there . . . check in with me next week?" Shan said, ringing off.

In the days and nights that followed, in counterpoint to the ocean, Beth filled the quiet with words that did not come easily at first.

But there they were. Real. Fact. A record. Testimony. His, her own, and of course, to friendship.

THE END

A NOTE ON
HISTORICAL REFERENCES

How to Be a Revolutionary is a work of fiction.

The quote from W. H. Auden's poem "As I walked out one evening" is used gratefully with the permission of Penguin Random House LLC, and with permission of Curtis Brown, Ltd. The English translation of a Du Fu poem, translated by Stephen Owen, is used gratefully with permission of Palgrave and Stephen Owen.

All quotes from newspaper articles in this novel are fictional. Any historical person that is portrayed in this novel is from the historical record, but all conversations and correspondence in the form of letters are the author's own creations.

The letters between Langston Hughes and a South African writer are entirely invented. Two sections of Langston Hughes's testimony are taken directly from recorded transcripts and reflect his own words (on pages 175, 176 and 177): *Testimony of Langston Hughes (accompanied by his counsel, Frank D. Reeves) before the Senate Permanent Subcommittee on Investigations of the Committee on Government Operations, Tuesday, March 24, 1953.* The rest of the Senate testimony has been fictionalized by the author.

The author gratefully acknowledges the book that inspired the fictional character Zhao: Yang Jisheng, *Tombstone: The Untold Story of Mao's Great Famine* (London: Allen Lane, 2012) and also the usefulness of the following texts: Ma Jian, *Beijing Coma* (New York: Farrar, Straus and Giroux, 2008); Langston Hughes and Arnold Rampersad, *I Wonder as I Wander: An Auto-biographical Journey* (New York: Penguin Random House, 2011); Langston Hughes, *Langston Hughes and the South African Drum Generation (The Correspondence)* (London: Palgrave, 2010); Etsuko Taketani, "'Spies and Spiders' Langston Hughes and the Transpacific Dragnets" (*The Japanese Journal of American Studies*, No. 25, 2014); Arnold Rampersad, *The Life of Langston Hughes: Volume I: 1902–1941, I, Too, Sing America* (Oxford: Oxford University Press, 2002); Daniel Won-gu Kim, "'We, Too, Rise with You': Recovering Langston Hughes's African (Re)Turn 1954–1960 in *An African Treasury,* the *Chicago Defender,* and *Black Orpheus*" (*African American Review,* Vol. 41, No. 3, Fall, 2007).

My gratitude to my agent Anjali Singh who has remained ever-present and ever-determined, the team at Aisha Pande Literary, my editor Andy Hsiao who read and edited the text exactly how I'd hoped, everyone at Verso Books, especially Cian McCourt and Duncan Ranslem, my early readers, including Kelwyn Sole, Rejane Woodroffe and Mapule Mohulatsi. Thank you to Nadia Davids for the poem. My eternal thanks to my mother and the rest of my family, my friends, and special thanks to Milan and Jetten, as always.